The Hostile Country

Twin Ranchos was a hell-town in the lusty, brawling days that followed the Civil War, a town that wanted no law and order. It had been a backwater and a ghost town – until the yellow metal had been found in the hills and in the tumbling rivers close by. Men came from all parts to mine the gold, to pan the rivers, and where there was gold, there were greedy, ruthless men ready to take it with one hand and shoot to kill with the other.

No man, they said, could tame a town like that. The last man to try had been shot down in his room; wakened from sleep to hear the crash of glass, to see the round black hole of the .45 and the spurt of flame, to feel the leaden impact of the slug in the split second before he died.

Then Rod Wellman rode into town, seeking the man who had killed his brother . . . .

The Hostile Country

Peter J. Kerman

 **A Black Horse Western**

ROBERT HALE · LONDON

© 1967, 2002 John Glasby
First hardcover edition 2002
Originally published in paperback as
The Hostile Country by Chuck Adams

ISBN 0 7090 7210 4

Robert Hale Limited
Clerkenwell House
Clerkenwell Green
London EC1R 0HT

Typeset by
Derek Doyle & Associates, Liverpool.
Printed and bound in Great Britain by
Antony Rowe Limited, Wiltshire

ONE
Gold Trail

In the harsh, glaring heat of high noon, the five men rode
slowly into the widening in the canyon that was the site of
one of the old mines. Jed Carson and Syd Littlejohn rode
side by side, a few yards behind the tall, straight figure of
Hank Wellman, Sheriff of Twin Ranchos. Further back,
bringing up the rear, were Will Denver and Lee Elston.
Half a mile behind there had been rock slides, cutting into
the walls of the canyon, narrowing it, forcing them to ride
in single file and the men had not yet closed up again.

The day before, they had followed the tracks across the
desert and had spent the night five miles below the mine
site near one of the few waterholes in the harsh alkali.
Before it had grown fully light that morning, Wellman had
gone on ahead of the others to study the situation around
the mine. There had been little doubt in his mind that the
site was deserted and that the gang had ridden on, were
doubtless holed up among the rocks at the head of the
trail where they could cover the whole spread of trail.

Carson felt his hands perspiring on the reins and
rubbed them on his shirt nervously. He did not share
Wellman's belief that Booth and his men had ridden on
up the trail. There was an itch between his shoulder blades
and the feel of eyes on him, of a finger tightening on the

5

trigger of a rifle as a hidden marksman drew a bead on him from the cover of one of the wooden shacks which stood out clearly now in the sunlight, slanting into the canyon. One of the windows winked with the sunlight as he stared at it and he blinked his eyes several times, running a dry tongue over equally dry lips. He let his gaze flicker back to Wellman.

'You reckon he's right about 'em havin' moved up to the top of the trail?' he asked softly, turning to Littlejohn as he spoke, lowering his voice so that Wellman did not hear.

'Could be. Don't see any sign of 'em near the shacks.' Littlejohn looked up the slope, lips tight.

'I was wonderin' if they might be lyin' in wait for us. We're nearly in range now. A Winchester could pick us off from here.'

'It's more'n three hundred yards. They'd have to be dead-eyes to hit a man from that range. Besides, I figure that Wellman wouldn't be ridin' up like that if there was much chance of any of 'em being in the mine.'

When they rode close enough to the shacks for a rifle-man to pick them off without any trouble and there was still no shot from any of the buildings, Carson felt a little easier in his mind. He was still unhappy about riding the full length of the trail and drawing fire deliberately from the rocks which overlooked it, but he had been sworn in as a deputy for this job by Wellman and he couldn't very well back out of it now. They rode past the wooden cyanide baths, past the shacks which stood against one side of the rock face. No sign of movement inside any of them. The little tingle between Carson's shoulder blades grew stronger and more persistent. He kept his eyes on the nearest shack, letting his horse pick its way forward slowly now, his right hand hovering over the butt of the gun in its holster. The boards of the shack were now bleached almost white by the long years of strong sunlight and he noticed that the dust in the doorway had not been disturbed at all by prints of any kind. He let his breath sigh out of his lungs. Ahead of them, the trail narrowed swiftly. A swift-rushing stream gushed from the side of the rock some fifty feet above the trail and tumbled in a sparkling column across their path.

Wellman reined up his mount, turned to face them as they rode slowly up to him. There was a grim expression on his lean, tanned features. 'There's a long open stretch up the slope to those rocks yonder,' he said softly. 'I reckon they must be there, watchin' us this minute, probably waitin' for us to get within killing distance before they open up on us.' He grinned faintly, let his keen gaze wander over them, one at a time. 'Any of you want to back out now?'

Carson sat taut in the saddle. If any of the others had spoken up at that moment he would have nodded his head, but they were all silent and the opportunity for him to back out was lost.

'All right. Then string out into a line, keep your rifles ready and shoot at anythin' that moves. Those *hombres* up there won't be wastin' ammunition when they do open up.'

'How do you figure we can get up there without bein' killed, Sheriff?' asked Elston. He sat with his shoulders hunched forward, one arm resting on the saddlehorn. 'No cover there for the last fifty yards or so. Besides, there's a backtrail yonder over the ledge where they can slip away if we do manage to pin 'em down.'

Wellman nodded. 'We'll get a man around there. Carson! You reckon you can get up there and watch the end of that ledge? If they start anythin' we'll cover you from here.'

'I guess so.' Carson lifted his head, shielded his eyes from the direct glare of the sun, nodded as he tried to visualise the country which lay behind the ledge and the long, circuitous trail which would lead up to it. He pressed his lips together into a tight line, considering. 'Reckon it might take a couple of hours though, to work my way up there.'

'We've got to close the back door,' Wellman said. 'Better get started.'

Carson looked again at the rocky heights, then shrugged, gigged his mount away from the trail and rode up into the rocks, unsheathing the Winchester as he did so. Wellman waited until the other was out of sight, then motioned the rest of the posse forward, keeping his eyes on the narrow track ahead. The ground underfoot was now of loose shale and sand which shifted treacherously and when the strung-out line of men were less than a hundred yards along the slope the crack of a rifle sent Wellman's mount lunging wildly to one side. Savagely, he pulled on the reins, hauled it to one side, then slid from the saddle and rolled behind the sheltering rocks close at hand. The rest of the men were down and crouched behind the boulders by the time the second bullet kicked up a spurt of dust less than three feet away.

Easing himself forward a little, Wellman called loudly. 'You don't have a chance, Booth. Come out with your hands lifted and the rest of your men with you.'

The only answer was another shot and the bullet clipped the boulder near his face sending chips of stone rattling over his head and shoulders as he pulled himself down sharply.

'All right, Booth, if that's the way you want it,' Wellman shouted, his words echoing back at him from the surrounding rocks. 'We've got you bottled up here, so I guess we can outwait you. Mebbe a few hours in the sun will make you change your mind.'

Littlejohn grumbled something from close by, then looked back up the slope and said harshly: 'Knowin' Booth, he'll have food and water up there, Hank. We won't be able to starve him out.'

'Mebbe not. But we've got a mite more shade down here than they have and it's goin' to be a long, hot afternoon,' Wellman answered. 'Booth's got a short patience and judgin' by that, we oughtn't to have long to wait before he tries to make a break for it.'

Burning waves of heat rolled over the sun-glistening

rocks all about them as the afternoon wore on. There was a thick, tangible silence hanging over everything, so deep and still that it was possible to hear the click of a rifle bolt from the rocks above them as one of the outlaws levered a shell into his rifle. They cooked their meal in one of the shacks a couple of hundred yards down the trail, Denver remaining in the shack, preparing the food while each man in turn took his chance at a quick run back, risking a bullet on the way.

'You reckon it's any worse up there than it is down here?' muttered Elston thickly. He ground the stub of a cigarette into the sand in front of him, wiped the sweat from his forehead with the back of his hand.

'Sure it is,' grunted Wellman tightly. 'They ain't got any cover up there like we have. This is little enough, I'll grant you, but it keeps us out of the direct sunlight. By now, they'll be close to fryin' up there.'

He paused, leaned a little to one side at a sudden sound from the rocks some fifty yards above them, then cupped his hands to his mouth. 'Booth! You'd better come down and give yourselves up. We can stick it out here as long as need be.'

'You ain't taking any of us in, lawman!' yelled a harsh voice which Wellman recognized as belonging to Booth. 'The first one of you who tries to get up the trail draws a bullet.'

Wellman sighed, shrugged his shoulders as he turned a sweat-stained face towards Elston. 'Reckon we're in for a long wait,' he said tautly. 'But at least we know where they are.'

'How many men do you figure he's got with him?'

'Hard to say. There were six of 'em when they lit out of town. We shot one and wounded a couple of others. They're probably up there now.'

'Could be they'll be the first to break,' suggested Littlejohn. He licked his dry lips, rubbed the muscles at the back of his neck.

'Could be. This sun won't help a wounded man to stay

patient, even if Booth has a gun on him to stop him from
tryin' to run.'

For the rest of the long afternoon and evening, they
remained holed up among the rocks, the sweat boiling out
of their bodies, cramp seizing their legs, the glare,
refracted from the boulders, half-blinding them. Wellman
thrust his legs out straight behind him to ease the dragging pincers of agony which laced through them, sucked
in a deep gust of air and squinted up at the line of rocks
above them, where the last red rays of the setting sun were
touching the summit with long fiery fingers of scarlet and
crimson. Darkness would move in soon and if it was possible, he wanted to take Booth and the rest of his men
before then. Here, there were many places where a man
might slip through the trail without being seen and the
overpowering heat of the day had taken its toll of the men
with him. He knew that none of them relished the idea of
shooting it out with that bunch of killers above them, that
they were only staying there with him for fear of being
branded as cowards once they got back to Twin Ranchos.

His mouth twisted as he let the thoughts run through
his mind. Maybe he had been a fool to take the job of
Sheriff in a hell-town iike Twin Ranchos. There had been
precious little law and order when he had ridden into
this prairie town some four months before. Ten years
earlier, it had been a brawling place of saloons and
whiskey bars, of dance halls and gambling dens, run by
men whose greed had built up the town into a place of
death and fear. But then, with the great migration westward, the frontier had been pushed further and further
beyond Twin Ranchos and once again, it had become a
backwater, a ghost-town, peopled by a handful of men,
too old to move. Not until gold had been discovered in
these hills had life returned to the town. Now it was filled
with men of a deadlier breed than those earlier outlaws,
men who held human life cheaply, who killed for the
sheer savage pleasure of it, robbing and looting, stealing
and cheating. Such men as Matt Booth and the killers

who associated with him, a dangerous gang of outlaws.

Wellman was the law in Twin Ranchos, a man who knew all about violence, who had lived with it ever since he had run away from his father's ranch twelve years before, determined to make his own way in the world. He had been in town less than a month when shooting had broken out in one of the saloons and, forced to defend himself, had shot down two of the most brutal killers in the territory, men who claimed to be fast with a gun. The county Sheriff had offered him the job of town Sheriff on the spot when he had heard of the shooting and now he was here, with this handful of men he had sworn in as deputies, crouched down among these rocks, risking his neck for the sake of the decent people in Twin Ranchos and for the pay of two hundred dollars a month which went with the job.

Lifting his head cautiously, he scanned the host of creeping shadows in the broken land all about them. The tricky overtones of dusk in this rugged country and the faint breeze which lifted the dust and stirred the branches of the few stunted pines and bushes, endowed every shadow with a human form. As he strained to listen, he thought he heard a faint scraping from somewhere directly above him and tried to push his vision into the tangled mass of rocks and boulders which marked the spot where he reckoned Booth and the others were holed up.

Desperately, he tried to separate fact from phantasy in his mind, knowing that during this transitional period between daylight and darkness, every sense could be deceptive and a man could not always believe what he saw and heard. From below him, Denver came out of the doorway of one of the wooden mine shacks, paused for a second, then called up in a low tone: 'You coverin' me, Wellman?'

'Sure. Come on up.' Strained and frazzled nerves were beginning to get the better of them, Wellman thought to himself as he watched Denver come up the steep slope at a scuttling run, bobbing and weaving from side to side,

expecting a bullet at any moment to come seeking him
out from the rocks. Denver came crawling up to the shallow gully where the others were crouched, sliding his rifle
in front of him, the metal rasping on the rocks, the sound
grating on Wellman's taut nerves.

'You see anything, Sheriff?'

Wellman shook his head. 'Thought I heard somethin' a
few moments ago, but it could have been my imagination.
You get to thinkin' you hear a lot of things when it's quiet
like this.'

'You sure he can't have slipped off, back into the rocks?'

'Not with Carson watchin' that stretch of the ledge. If
he's still awake.' Wellman made an effort to keep his voice
under control. The possibility that Booth knew this country far better than he did and did know of a way back
through the rocks had been nagging at him for almost two
hours now and the more he turned it over in his mind, the
more probable it seemed to him. He reached a sudden
decision.

'Littlejohn. Get up there along the side of the ledge
and see if you can spot anythin' moving yonder. From that
rock there you should be able to see along that ridge and
make out anybody there. We'll cover you from here.'

Littlejohn stared at him for a full minute as though on
the point of refusing. Then he licked his lips dryly, scram-
bled to his feet and began edging his way sideways, tilting
the brim of his hat a little against the strengthening breeze
which had sprung up with the setting of the sun and was
now whipping little flurries of sand and dust into their
faces. Wellman watched tensely as the other moved from
one boulder to another and there was something in that
motion which struck him instantly as familiar. Panic, that
was what it was, he reflected. The other was afraid, knowing that from where Booth and the others were holed up,
it would be possible for them to shoot down on him without showing themselves.

Littlejohn reached the end of the ledge, paused for a
moment, judging the distance across the stretch of open

ground to the boulder where he would be able to look along the upslanting ridge behind which Booth and the others were hiding. Then he got his legs under him, took heart in the fact that his upgrade climb had brought no shots whistling from the overhanging rocks, and lunged forward, the barrel of his rifle glinting in the faint light that showed between the rocks. A couple of rifles barked from the upper ledge. Wellman caught a fragmentary glimpse of dust kicked up at Littlejohn's heels as he ran desperately for cover. Then he staggered just as he reached the shelter of the boulder, fell the last couple of feet, legs going from under him.

Wellman swore softly under his breath. From that distance it had been impossible to tell how badly hit the other had been, or whether he was still alive. He could just make out the shape of the other's boots sticking out from behind the boulder. Then, as he watched, he saw them being withdrawn into cover and knew that Littlejohn was still alive, although he might have been hit bad by that second bullet.

'They're still there,' muttered Denver harshly, 'and there's nothin' wrong with their aim either.'

'We've got to move up,' Wellman grated. 'We can't hit them from down here and it ain't likely that they'll show themselves.'

'How do you figure on moving up when they can watch every inch of the trail from here up?' grunted the other, a faint trace of sarcasm in his tone. 'You saw what happened to Littlejohn. They must've spotted him leaving here and waited until he jumped across that open stretch of ground. He never had a chance.'

Wellman stared belligerently at the other for a long moment, lips drawn into a tight line across his grim features, then he said tightly: 'I'm going forward myself. Keep me covered. Shoot at anythin' that moves up there. If we wait until it's dark we'll lose 'em.'

Carefully, Wellman edged forward, keeping his head and shoulders down, exposing himself as little as possible.

He felt the tingling renewal of tension in his veins but even in the growing darkness, he had memorised every rock and ledge, picking his way noiselessly forward. The stunted cedar stands and bushes which grew out of the thin, arid soil among the rocks, afforded him a little cover, but he remembered what had happened to Littlejohn and moved slowly and cautiously. He had left his rifle behind, relying on the Colts in his holsters.

Soon, he was crouched down at the end of the shallow depression in the rocks. In front of him lay the open space across which Littlejohn had moved when that slug had hit him. He narrowed his eyes and tried to make out the other among the rocks, then spotted him huddled against the smooth face of the rocky wall at his back. His face was just visible as a grey blur in the dimness.

'You hit bad, Littlejohn?' he called softly.

He saw the other start at the sudden sound of his voice, then the man edged forward a couple of inches, peering at him. 'Bullet in the shoulder,' he called back. 'They're watchin' this stretch of ground. Better stay there.'

'Can you see 'em from there?'

There was a brief pause as the other pushed himself up slowly onto his knees, lifting his head an inch at a time. His hard-boned length pressed tightly against the boulder in front of him. After a brief survey of the territory in front of his position, he turned his head. 'Somethin' there, but I can't make out how many.'

'Stay there. Shoot if you see anything move.'

'Sure thing Sheriff.'

Sucking air down into his lungs Wellman tensed, sprang upward and forward in the same movement, his clawing fingers just getting a touch on the rocky ledge in front of him. There was the sharp bark of a rifle close by. He felt the wind of the bullet near his cheek, saw the orange flash of the weapon in the dimness, threw himself tightly against the hard rock, drew his Colt and fired in a blur of motion. The scream cut like the lash of a whip through the dusk. Out of the edge of his vision, Wellman saw the man lurch forward from where he had been poised on a narrow ledge. Then he fell like a sack of beans, crashing onto the ground six feet below.

Wellman lay quite still. A moment later, he heard what he had been listening for. Across the narrow canyon which stretched away ahead of him, down a piece from where he stood and slightly above the level of his own head, he heard the faint rustle of a man's harsh breathing in the darkness, the sound a man made when he was feeling uncomfortable and uneasy. Although he could not see the man, Wellman knew exactly where he was. A man with an ambush on his mind would be either holed up in a cleft in the rocks, or lying on top of a ledge overlooking the floor of the canyon. From the position of the man's breathing it was obvious he was lying on the low ledge and in this position, he would have a very restricted position in which to lie. He should be lying face downward, propped on his elbows, with his rifle between his hands, peering into the darkness which now lay thick and black in the canyon.

Glancing about him, Wellman tried to make out any of the others, knowing that they would be somewhere in the vicinity, alerted now by the shot which had killed one of their number. Softly, he padded across to the other side of the canyon, felt with his outstretched fingers for the smooth wall of rock on that side, reached up until his hooked fingers caught at the ledge. He could hear the man almost as obviously as if he could be seen. His head was probably protruding over the edge of the ledge because there could not be too much room up there and he would want to peer in every direction.

Guided by the sound, he inched his way along the wall, pressing himself in as close as possible. The other would be watching for him still on the other side, knowing that it had been from there that the shot had come which had killed his companion. A stone rattled onto the floor of the canyon as the hidden gunman shifted his arms. Wellman grinned viciously to himself. The other was getting nervous, wondering where he was.

A few seconds later, the man said hoarsely: 'Can you see that *hombre*, Booth?'

Wellman waited tautly. If the outlaw leader answered, it would give him a clue as to where the other was in the darkness. But there was a long moment of silence following the other's whisper and Wellman knew that Booth did not intend to give away his position until he knew exactly where he was.

Picking his way forward, Wellman moved along the rocky wall until he was directly beneath the sound of heavy breathing. It seemed incredible that he could be so close to the man without being seen. Not until the other moved was he able to make him out, a vaguely seen blur, visible only against the lighter hue of the sky showing above the canyon.

For a moment, he remained there, taut and tensed, then he sprang upwards, his fingers hooked, clawing at the man's neck. He felt his nails dig deep into the soft flesh of the man's throat, tightened his grip, cutting off the man's cry before it could be uttered. Lifting his feet from the ground, he threw the whole of his weight on the other, felt the man slide over the rim of the ledge, unable to help himself. His rifle fell from his fingers, struck Wellman on the shoulder and then dropped onto the rough ground with an audible clatter. There was no time to be lost now. Savagely, he brought the gunman crashing from his perch. Not wishing to lose the other in the darkness, he maintained his hold on the man's throat, rolled him over onto his back and went down with his knees on the man's chest, pinning him to the rocks. The man threshed and struggled furiously, hands caught around the Sheriff's wrists, straining to pull them apart, away from his neck.

Even though taken by surprise and winded by the fall, the gunman was still strong and they rolled over and over as the other suddenly thrust up with his knee, catching Wellman on the thigh, knocking him over onto his side.

Wellman took a few savage kicks to his leg in the

attempt to re-establish superiority, then got astride the other once more. Realising the Sheriff's murderous intent, the man braced himself on his elbows on the ground, struggling to throw him off. Somehow, he managed to wrest Wellman's hands from around his throat, pulled in a gust of air and opened his mouth to give a sharp yell of warning to the others.

At once, Wellman lashed out with his bunched fist, caught the man flush on the mouth and the yell died into a gurgling scream which carried only a short distance, as the killer's head was jerked around. In almost the same instant, there was a hoarse cry from the trail some distance away.

'He's gettin' away, Sheriff! Booth – he's escapin'.'

Several seconds fled before Wellman recognized Carson's voice from along the trail. Then came the bark of three shots, following close on each other, the tight, atro-phying echoes chasing each other down the canyon. Taking advantage of this sudden and unexpected diver-sion, the gunman heaved up with all of his strength, succeeded in hurling Wellman against the rocky canyon wall. An out-thrusting piece of rock caught him on the side of the head, half-stunning him and in the haze of pain, he saw the gunman clamber to his feet, stand sway-ing for a moment as he pulled air down into his aching lungs, rubbing his jaw as he reached down for his rifle, fingers scrabbling for it. Desperately, Wellman shook his head. A fresh stab of agony lanced through it as he clawed for the Colt at his waist. Levelling it, he triggered it twice, saw the man buck and stagger as the bullets hit home.

The muffled sound of hoofbeats reached him as he moved forward. A horse whinnied in the distance, there came the sound of another gunshot and then silence. Denver came charging hotfoot up the slope, with Littlejohn moving in at his heels, one hand clutching at his wounded shoulder, the other holding his gun tightly.

Wellman wheeled sharply, pointed along the canyon, almost sliding onto his face in the treacherous layer of dust. 'Get down there!' he yelled harshly.

They ran down the slope, between the rocky walls. Bursting out into the open, Wellman stared about him. There was a solitary figure making its way up the slope towards them, occasionally running, at other times, edging forward carefully.

Denver lifted his gun and took a quick aim, finger tightening on the trigger, then paused as Wellman called: 'Hold your fire! It's Carson.'

Carson came up to them, breathing heavily. He thrust his gun back into its holster. 'I couldn't help it, Sheriff,' he said defensively. 'He was on me before I knew it. I heard the shootin' and came up to investigate. He must've jumped on his mount by then because the first I knew he was bearin' down on me along the trail, aimin' his horse straight at me. I got off a couple of shots at him and I reckon I may have hit him but —'

'Save it,' said Wellman harshly. 'Ain't no sense in tryin' to follow him in this darkness. He knows every back trail there is in this territory and we'd likely break our horses' legs down there if we went after him. You sure he was alone?'

'Saw nobody else,' muttered the other. 'You reckon that —' Before he could get any more words out, there was a savage burst of firing from the rocks at their backs and Wellman knew that not all of the men with Booth had either got away with him or been killed.

Three shots . . . a fourth. Then the posse were firing back, aiming at the orange splashes of flame from the guns of the outlaws. A man let up a tremendous shout in the midst of darkness and gunfire as a bullet found its mark. Ricochets whined in murderous chorus off the rocks. Then it was all over. One of the outlaw gang tried to get away down the slope, running and sliding, rolling over and over in the dirt, heading for the shacks close by the mine. A volley of gunfire cut after him, sent him plummeting forward onto his face, finishing up near the well which had been sunk in the solid rock near the trail.

Wellman thrust his gun back into leather. He stood there in the deep stillness, listening to the high wind keening among the rocks, rustling the still branches of the cedars and mesquite. There was a deep restlessness bubbling in him which he tried to hold down within himself. He ought to feel satisfied that he had broken the Booth gang and killed so many of its members. But the thought of Matt Booth, still out there on the loose, somewhere in the night, disturbed him more than he cared to admit.

Slowly, he walked down the winding trail towards the spot where they had left their horses, tethered near the mine shacks. Shadows moved around the old, deserted buildings. The grating rustle of the wind as it caught the sand and flung it against the wooden walls caught his ears. Each nightfall, this country seemed to come to life, he thought wearily.

They rode back into Twin Ranchos around four o'clock the following afternoon, with the bodies of the slain outlaws over the saddles of their mounts. Wellman tied his bay in front of the Sheriff's office and walked wearily up the steps, opening the door and stepping inside while the posse took the bodies to the undertaker. He walked slowly into the office, moving with the stiffness of a man who had been in the saddle for several days, seated himself in the chair behind the desk, opened a drawer, and pulled out a bottle of whiskey and a glass. Pouring himself a drink, he sat forward in his chair, rested his elbows on the table, and stared at the golden liquid in the glass, lost in thought. He was hungry, he was thirsty and he felt dead beat, the solution of all three was before him and yet he was unsure which to do first. Finally, he reached out, lifted the glass to his lips and drank the whiskey down in a single gulp. It burned the back of his throat, but the warmth in his stomach made him feel a lot better. It felt good just to be able to sit there and think of nothing for a little while. Sit down and stretch your legs, he thought idly, lean back and rest your shoulders, then pour another drink and sip that one a little more slowly than the first.

The late afternoon sunlight slanted in through the dusty window that looked out onto the street. He listened with only half an ear to the sound of men riding past the window, footsteps on the creaking wooden slats of the boardwalk outside the office. Then footsteps stopped right outside the door, a hand tried the handle and then the door was thrown open and the portly figure of Hal Kerby, the mayor of Twin Ranchos came in, looked around the room for a moment before resting his eyes on him. Closing the door, he came inside, rubbing his hands together as though washing them. His florid features glistened with sweat but although the weather had been stifling hot during the whole of the day, he still insisted on wearing his full dress, with the neck of his shirt buttoned right up and the cravat showing boldly, exactly in the centre.

'Just saw you ride into town, Sheriff,' he said thickly, lowering himself into the other chair. 'Fine job you did, running that gang to earth. Reckon we've been needing a Sheriff like you for some time. If you'd happened along a year or so ago when this town really started booming again, I think it might have stopped a lot of trouble.'

Wellman sighed. 'It's been a long day,' he said; 'and we let Booth slip through our fingers.'

'Booth got away?' For a moment, there was an almost incredulous surprise in the other's voice. Then he shrugged his broad shoulders massively. 'He won't bother us again, take my word for it. He'll ride and keep on riding, taking any old trail that will get him out of the territory. Without his men to back him up, he's finished.'

'I wish I could feel as sure of that.' Wellman sipped his second drink, watching the other closely over the rim of the glass. 'I figure it's more likely that he'll ride on for a little way until he can get more men around him. Then he'll head back for revenge and he isn't likely to make the same mistake a second time. He'll get more men than he had before and the next time we'll find it even harder to fight him.'

Kerby took out a slim black cheroot from one of his pockets, bit off the end and spat it onto the floor, then struck a match and waved the flame across the end, inhaling as he did so until the cheroot was well alight. Blowing smoke into the air, he tilted his head back and said quietly: 'Even if you are right, Wellman, it will still take him a little while to find men who'll follow him. A man who lets himself be trapped in the hills and all of his men shot isn't likely to command much respect among the type of men he needs to back him up. I think we can take it that his power here has been broken for some time to come thanks to you and the men who rode out with you.'

'I hope you're right.' He finished his drink, set the empty glass down in front of him. 'But there are others in town who think the same way as he did. I'd better make my rounds.'

'Of course.' Kerby placed his podgy hands on the arms of the chair and thrust himself to his feet with an obvious effort. He took out a red kerchief and wiped the sweat from his features. Shambling towards the door, he opened it, then paused and looked back. 'I met Littlejohn on my way here, he's over at the Doc's getting that shoulder of his fixed.'

Wellman nodded, waited until the other had left, then hitched up the heavy gunbelt a little higher, checked the shells in the guns, and went out into the street once more, unhitching the bay from the rails and swinging up into the saddle. There was a coolness in the air that flowed along the main street now, a wind that came down from the tops of the mountains and already the setting sun was throwing long shadows across the street. From one of the saloons came the sound of raucous voices raised in song while a tinny piano tried to sound above the shouting. Probably some of the prospectors had come into town with their supply of yellow dust and things were just beginning to hot up before the business of fleecing them began. He smiled grimly to himself as he rode slowly along the centre of the dusty street, holding the reins lightly in his right hand.

He knew that he was drawing curious glances from the boardwalks, but this was a ritual he went through every day he happened to be in town, this riding the rounds of the streets and alleys of Twin Ranchos, letting everybody know he was there, showing himself, bringing home to them all that there was now law and order in the town. By now, the news of what had happened to Matt Booth and his gang would have spread throughout the town and would be the talking point on everybody's lips. Things might be more quiet and subdued tonight. Anybody thinking of making trouble might pause and consider, remembering what had happened to Booth, knowing that the same thing might happen to them.

In the beginning, after he had first been given the post of Sheriff, several of the town's citizens had warned him of this dangerous practice of riding the streets alone just before dark, telling him that he was asking for a bullet from an unlit alley, that he was risking his life every time he rode out like this, making a target of himself for any outlaw who happened to be in town. But now it had become a nightly thing and he relied on his instincts to give him that split second warning of trouble.

Circling the perimeter of the town, he rode back into the main street. There were a few lights on in the windows of one or two of the stores now, he noticed. Several of the shops were being locked up for the night and he noticed Callon, the banker, making his way over to the hotel for his evening meal. Everything seemed to be normal.

Reining his mount in front of the small restaurant next to the livery stable, he went inside. Here every lamp shone with a full yellow brightness. Opening the door, he looked about him. It was early yet and only three of the tables there were occupied. Picking out one where he could watch the door and the window overlooking the street at the same time, he settled back in his chair, gave his order to Miguel, and waited for it to be served up to him.

When it came Miguel set it out in front of him, then hovered close to his chair, a grin on his brown features. 'They say that you catch Señor Booth in the mountains, Sheriff,' he said eagerly. 'He is dead, *sí?*'

Wellman shook his head slowly. 'He is dead – no,' he replied. 'He managed to get away while we were taking care of the others.'

'That is bad.' The other shrugged, brightened. 'Still, with all of his men dead, his teeth have been drawn. There is little he can do now.'

'I hope so, Miguel. I certainly do.'

Miguel hesitated, then went back to his place behind the bar where he stood, mopping the counter with a wet cloth. A few more customers came in a while later. Slowly, the place was filling up. Wellman knew most of the men here. A sprinkling of prospectors from the hills, just in town, anxious for a spending spree. It would not be long before they had lost every grain of gold for which they had panned and dug more than six months, working out their lives in rugged fastnesses of the hills, just so that they might spend a few hours in town, getting drunk enough to forget the long, sun-scorched days and frost-filled nights, drunk enough not to see when they were being cheated at poker.

Finishing his meal, he sat back, rolled and lit a cigarette, smoking it slowly, feeling the warmth of the place flow into him, loosening the taut muscles of his body, making him feel good. Maybe Booth had fled the territory and might even be heading for the border at that very moment, all of his dreams of taking over the town turned to dust in his mouth now that his men had been smashed and killed.

Out in the street, he walked his mount along to the livery stables, placed it in one of the rear stalls, saw that it had plenty of feed and water, then stepped out onto the shadowed boardwalk. Thoughtfully, he made his way back to the office, locked it up for the night, then stepped across to the small hotel where he had his room on the ground floor. It seemed an eternity since he had slept in a real bed, out on the trail which led after the Booth gang, and although he was used to sleeping rough, he sometimes, as now, felt the urge for clean, smooth sheets against his tired body.

Climbing the creaking steps into the hotel, he nodded to the sleepy clerk behind the desk in the lobby, took his key and made his way wearily to his room. Sinking down onto the edge of the bed, he stared moodily out of the window. Most of the lights were on along the whole length of the street now that it was getting dark. The sun had disappeared behind the tall range of hills to the west of the town and the cool darkness had settled over everything. For a long while he sat there, staring out into the main street, watching the people on the boardwalks, their features alternately caught by the slanting beams of light from the windows of the buildings overlooking the street, and then plunged into darkness and anonymity as they passed on into the shadows.

Pulling off his boots, he tossed them into one corner of the room. Saddleworn and stiff, he stretched himself out on the low, iron bed, listening to the usual night sounds of Twin Ranchos outside the window. If there was no trouble during the night which couldn't be handled by Charlie Ferris, the deputy he had left in charge of the town while he had been away on the trail of Matt Booth, he ought to be able to grab himself a decent night's sleep. Maybe that was too much to hope for, he told himself tiredly, as he clasped his hands at the back of his neck and stared up at the ceiling.

He still felt uncommonly troubled by the fact that Booth had succeeded in getting away from them in spite of the cordon he had set up on the trail, but if the gunman did decide to head back to Twin Ranchos, possibly for the purpose of revenge, it would take him some time to collect together enough men to back his play and even Wellman did not consider the other man fool enough to ride back and try it alone. Booth might be angry and thirsting for vengeance on the man who had broken his power in the territory, but he was not stupid.

It was still dark inside the room when he awoke, startled by some sudden sound that had reached down into that subconscious part of him which never slept. For several seconds, he lay there on the bed, trying to figure out the source of that sound which had woken him, straining to pick it out again. Silence lay thick and heavy about him.

Then, abruptly, before he was aware of the danger, the glass of the window was shattered by the butt of a pistol, wielded against it. A gust of cold night air sighed into the room, flooded about him. Instinctively, he started up from the bed, right hand clawing for the gun in the belt which hung on the edge of the chair. There was a hoarse laugh from outside the window, a splash of orange flame from the muzzle of the .45, then the brief impact of the slug that tore into his heart.

TWO
The Devil's
Gunman

Starting where the alkali desert left off, the rangeland began as an area of tufted, tough grass growing in patches out of the bare, arid ground. There was still plenty of the white alkali dust over the region, doing its best to smother the grass before it got root, the desert trying to encroach onto the range. Each year, it seemed, with the rainfall an unpredictable thing, the desert grew stronger and threatened to increase its hold on the territory between the wastelands and the high mountains.

Rod Wellman knew nothing of this country, but there was supposed to be a town somewhere close by according to the small party of prospectors he had met a couple of days before, and he knew that the broad trail which led him over the desert, would eventually take him to the town. The worst of the day's heat was past now and he rode straight and tall in the saddle, with a rider's looseness about him, sitting well forward to ease the burden on the horse. They had ridden hard all day, and the horse was tired, but it was a thoroughbred and he knew it could carry him for the rest of the day and well into the coming night if need be.

Shortly afterwards, the country began lifting from the flatness of the desert and he rode through a narrow cut, sheltered from sight on either side by its steep banks. Lips pressed tightly together, he stared ahead of him, his mind working ahead, bringing a tightness into his body, a taut sense of anticipation which had been growing steadily stronger since that day when he had received the telegram from a place called Twin Ranchos informing him that his brother, Hank, had been killed. There had been no further information concerning how Hank had died, just the simple statement that he was dead. Since then he had ridden more than five hundred miles to discover for himself what had happened.

He had not seen or heard from his brother for more than three years – and now this. He fingered the slip of paper in his pocket absently for a moment, moving his horse up the slope into the tall cedars at the top. In front of him, the country was cut up by rocky upthrusts and deep ravines and except for the rising quail and the running flight of a couple of longhorns, nothing moved in the deep stillness.

Half a mile on, he reined up, cast about him for any sign of alien life, saw nothing and dismounted. His fire was shielded by an overhang in a shallow rock cave and he knew it would not be seen by anyone else using this trail. Not that he had any fear of danger, but there was the indisputable fact that his brother had been killed and that could mean trouble in this stretch of the territory and he had no desire to ride into the middle of a range war, or something similar, until he knew what it was all about.

Breaking out food and utensils from his saddle pack, he knifed off a couple of slices of salt bacon with a deft handling of the long-bladed knife, spread them out on the bottom of the pan with a little grease and placed it over the fire to heat. The coffee pot was soon bubbling over the flames but before he ate, acting on the usual nervous urge to ensure that the surrounding terrain was scouted against any surprise attack, he made his way up to higher ground and examined every direction. He could see as far as the alkali, where it lay as a carpet of white in the distance to the east and far over to the west, where the sky was still red with the last glow of the sunset, the trail was a grey scar that wound over the low foothills, twisting in and out of the shadow-filled ravines. Finally satisfied that there was nothing to fear, he went back to the fire, seated himself with his back and shoulders against the rocky overhang and chewed reflectively on the bacon, washing it down with the hot coffee. At the moment, the knowledge of his brother's death formed only a vague emptiness in his mind. The anger would come and the desire for revenge when he found out what had happened. His brother had always been fast with a gun and he did not doubt that if he had been shot in cold blood, then whoever had done it, had caught him from ambush and not in fair fight.

He worked with the makings of a cigarette, lit it, drew the smoke gratefully into his lungs. There was a peacefulness here which he always seemed to feel at this time of the day; a deep and utter quiet that pressed in from the far horizons. During the minutes that he smoked the cigarette he tried to think things out, but failed. There were so many things he did not know, things he had to know before he could even make any sort of a plan in his own mind.

Although he had half-intended to make camp there for the night, he decided to ride onto into the nearest town. By degrees, the country become smoother, the grass more lush and once or twice, in the growing darkness, he spotted the dark shadows of herds on the lower slopes of the hills that lay a little to the north of him.

The yellow lights of the town showed themselves in the heart of the broad, sweeping valley as he topped a rise, set his mount to the downgrade. Hatchet Bend was a small town with no clearly defined road, merely a straggling trail that led in at one end and somehow managed to find its way out at the other, twisting in and out of the buildings scattered around a central square. Usually, the trail was a quagmire of mud whenever the rains came, but now, with no rain for close on a month, it was a dried-up river bed of grey dust which lifted in little whirls around his horse's hooves. He looked about him with a vaguely stirred interest as he walked his mount down the street, making a slow ride through the town. At intervals, on both right and left, there were intersections with the street, dark-mouthed alleys that ran off into mystery in utter blackness, with not a single light showing along any of them. Down each side of what passed for the main street, there were false-fronted erections of stout timber, leading back from the street itself to form wide boardwalks.

It was soon apparent that the town of Hatchet Bend boasted only one hotel and that was the single building in the entire town which had two stories. But there were four saloons which offered accommodation for a traveller and he decided on one of these, with the name 'Golden Trail Saloon' showing on a tattered wooden sign, the paint peeling from it where it had been scoured and abraded by wind and dust and rain. Outside the saloon was a peeled sapling hitching rail and he looked about him in vain for a livery stable.

Leaving the horse tethered to the rail, he pushed open the swing doors of the saloon and stepped inside, blinking his eyes automatically against the yellow glare of the oil lamps on the tables and hanging from the ceiling. The smell of smoke and stale tobacco hung heavily in the air and in places, above the tables in one or other of the corners of the room, the cigarette smoke hung in thick blue clouds above the men gambling or drinking there. It was a saloon like hundreds of others Rod Wellman had seen in his lifetime, neither better nor worse than most. There was a door to one side of the long bar which he guessed led into the sleeping quarters. In the interests of giving more space for tables and card playing, the bar was pressed hard against one side of the room, with scarcely enough room behind it for the two perspiring bartenders to move.

Walking over to the bar, Rod cast his eye over the other men bellied against it, their elbows braced on the polished mahogany, threw a quick glance in the cracked and chipped mirror that covered most of the wall at the back of it, let his gaze wander over the card players at the tables, paused for a moment as he noticed the two gunslicks seated by themselves at one of the tables. They, in turn, seemed to be more interested in him than they were in their drinks or the gamblers, but once they noticed his look on them, reflected in the mirror, they turned their heads away and began talking together in low tones over their drinks.

Giving his order to the bartender who came up, Rod waited until the bottle and glass had been set down in front of him, then said quietly: 'There a bed going for the night here?'

The bartender eyed him long and close for a moment, then said 'I guess we can fix you up, stranger. We don't usually get many trailmen like you here. More prospectors or those down on their luck who want a bed in this place. The others try the hotel across the street.'

'Tell him that's where he ought to go, Jed,' called a harsh voice behind Rod.

He turned slowly, pressing his shoulder blades against the edge of the bar. One of the gunslicks was eyeing him across the length of the room, a sneering grin on his face.

'You own this place, mister?' Rod asked quietly, his tone even, no emotion in it.

The other's grin widened, eyes narrowed viciously. Then the man shook his head. 'Don't own it, fella,' he said harshly. 'But we do like to know who's meanin' to stay here. You look like a lawman to me. Your face seems familiar.'

'As far as I recollect I ain't seen either of you two *hombres* before.' Without turning his attention from the men, aware that the card players had stopped their poker and were intent on watching what was happening, he said to the bartender: 'I still want that room and I reckon my money is as good as anybody else's in this room. Or is this the way you treat all strangers who ride into this town?'

The bartender did not answer him directly and almost deliberately, casually, Rod turned back to face him, knowing that he could watch the two men in the mirror at the back of the bar, see any moves they made. There was a film of perspiration now on the bartender's face which came neither from the work nor the heat in the room. He stood nervously twisting the moist cloth in his hands. Then he began to wipe the bar with it where Rod's glass had left a wet ring on the smooth wood.

'I guess you're as entitled to stay here as anybody.' he said finally, running the tip of his tongue around his lips. 'That is if you do have the money to pay.'

'I've got the money,' Rod said calmly. He tossed a handful of coins onto the bar. 'Will that cover it?'

The other stared down at the coins as though mesmerized, then nodded, his adam's apple bobbing nervously in his throat, a man still not sure that he was doing the right thing here, siding with this stranger who had ridden into town who was as yet an unknown quantity when it came to facing up to two gunmen such as those on the opposite side of the room.

'Sure, that'll cover it,' nodded the other tensely. He flickered a look towards the two men at the table. 'Have you got anythin' on this man, Ryan?'

'Just like to know what a man's business might be,' muttered the other fiercely. 'You can't be too careful these days. Could be a marshal out to make trouble for us.'

Rod lifted his head a little, assessed the other closely. The man's clothes were obviously trail-worn and dirty and he wore double-rigged gun gear with dark leather holsters, well-oiled, hugging his thighs, thonged around his legs. The butts of the Colts were smooth and well-worn and from either side of his nose, the narrowed eyes were pale and watery, filled with that strangely fanatical light of a killer. He was obviously a hardcase gunman on the prod for trouble, Rod decided; and his companion was of the same breed. Both men seemed to have been drinking for some time, but they were not drunk. They knew how to hold their liquor and what they had downed in the saloon would not slow nor mar their gunplay if they decided to make a showdown here.

'Are you a marshal, mister?' The sarcastic voice belonged to the other man at the table. He had an almost girlish face, but the cold eyes were like those of a snake and his hands were just a little too white around the knuckles where they rested on top of the table, close to the whiskey bottle in front of him.

'No,' Rod said quietly.

'Then what are you? And why are you in Hatchet Bend?'

'I figure that's somethin' which only concerns me,' said Rod mildly. 'At the moment, I'm here for a drink, a bite of supper and then a bed for the night. If you got any objection to that then you'd better put in your chips and find out anythin' else you want to know with a gun.'

The other laughed sneeringly, said loudly: 'That's the kind of approach that never varies. An entry into a saloon, a challenge and then a showdown. You got us all wrong, mister. We're just lookin' after our own interests.'

'Then don't make statements you have to back down from,' Rod said with a cold deliberateness. He poured himself a drink, saw the other half rise from his chair, his face white under the insult, one hand dropping a little towards the gun at his belt. Then he seemed to control himself and as his companion's hand came out to grab him around the wrist, he forced himself to relax and sank back into his chair.

'I'll fix you a bite of supper,' said the bartender quickly. He hurried away with a rapid backward glance at the two gunslicks, went through the door at the rear of the bar. Rod finished his drink, elbows leaning on the bar. When the bartender came back to tell him that the meal was ready and he could have it at one of the tables, he nodded, asked: 'Is there a livery stable in this godforsaken town where I can put up my horse?'

The other shook his head slowly. 'None now, mister. There was one, a little way down the street but this place has been a ghost-town for so long now that it's never been used. I can let you have some feed for your horse, but you'll have to keep him tethered outside for the night.'

Rod nodded, moved over to one of the empty tables in the corner. He attacked the food vigorously when it came, surprised to find how well cooked it was, far different from that which he had eaten on the trail. The two gunslicks did not seem to be paying any further attention to him, but he was still unsure as to whether or not they intended to make any play in the saloon. He had shown them up in front of the others and it was unlikely that they would take that insult without making some attack on him, although he reckoned they would wait until he was out in the street and could be a showdown from one of those unlit alleys.

Draining the last dregs of coffee from his cup, he glanced up to find that the bartender had moved over to his table, was standing close to his elbow.

'I've got a bed ready for you, mister,' he said loudly. 'There's a place through the back as soon as you're ready.'

'Thanks. I'll check my horse first.' Rod pushed back his chair, got to his feet.

In a low undertone, the barkeep said: 'Those two gunmen. Watch them, friend. They mean trouble for you.' Rod gave an almost imperceptible nod of his head as he brushed past the other. He had already made up his mind about that. There was a nagging little suspicion at the edge of his mind which he had been trying to force out into the open so that he might recognise it for what it was, but so far without any success. One of those men had said that his face seemed familiar to them and he racked his brains while he had been eating his supper, trying to recall if he had ever met up with either of them before, but although he had been around all along the frontier in the past two years, he could not remember either man, felt sure that they were mistaking him for someone else, which might

explain their behaviour in trying to needle him into a
gunfight.

Clapping his hat on top of his head, he walked towards
the door, threading his way among the tables, eyeing the
card players as he brushed past their table, then moved on
past where the two gunslicks were still drinking and talking together in low tones. They did not even glance up as
he moved past, and to all intents and purposes, it was as if
they had completely forgotten his presence there, but just
as he had moved a couple of feet past their table, he heard
the faint scrape of a chair on the rough sand floor. Slight
though the sound was, it was sufficient to warn him of
trouble and danger. Whirling, the guns jumping from
their holsters into his hands, he had them levelled on both
men just as they were rising to their feet behind the table,
their guns halfway out of their holsters. His fingers
squeezed the triggers and noise boomed in the confined
space of the roam. The cups in front of each man disinte-
grated into a shattered mass of coffee-soaked fragments as
the bullets smashed into them. The men jerked upright,
their eyes wide, the expressions on their faces telling more
plainly than words that they had never expected so fast a
draw, nor so quick a move from this man who towered
over them now, the smoke drifting from the muzzles of the
Colts held rock-steady in his hands, barrels lifted a little
until they were aligned on their chests.

Very gently, Rod drew back the hammers of the guns
with his thumbs, holding them there, ready to drop them
on the next chambers at a moment's notice. His lips were
drawn back a little over his teeth, his grin vicious and hard.

'That sure was a fool thing to try,' he grated harshly. His
gaze lowered to the guns still gripped in their hands. 'Now
either pull those guns all the way or let them go.'

Reluctantly almost, the men released their hold on the
weapons and they fell back into leather. Slowly, they sank
back into their chairs, not once removing their gaze from
his face.

'I reckon you both know I'd be within my rights to

shoot you down here and now for that stunt,' he murmured.

'Then why don't you?' rasped one of them tautly, the man named Ryan. 'You have the drop on us. Go ahead and pull the trigger, or is it that you don't shoot down men in cold blood?'

'Not usually,' Rod said calmly. 'But with rattlers who try to gun a man down behind his back, I'm willin' to forget.'

Ryan licked his lips dryly, reached out for the whiskey and splashed some into his glass, gulping it down hastily, spilling some onto his shirt. Some also dribbled from his lips onto his chin.

'You look disturbed, friend,' Rod said softly. He pulled the chair out with one hand after holstering one of the .45's, seated himself in it, still facing the two men. 'Supposin' you tell me what all this is about, why you tried to gun me down like that.'

'Just a little misunderstandin',' said the other man quickly. He glanced at his companion out of the corner of his eye, a warning glance which told the other to shut up and leave the talking to him. Watching the younger man, Rod wondered what it was they had to hide, knew that he would not be safe until he found out what it was for himself.

'You're lyin',' he snapped, boring his gaze into the other. 'Your friend reckoned he'd seen me someplace before. I'm pretty certain he hasn't. I'd like to know why he said that.'

'I made a mistake,' mumbled the other thinly. 'Anybody can do that, I reckon.'

'Seems a mighty peculiar mistake when you were ready to shoot me in the back for it.' Rod's tone was hard. He noticed the sheen of sweat greased on the man's forehead, running in little trickles down his grizzled cheeks. 'Do I remind you of somebody? Is that it?'

'No. That isn't it.' Ryan shifted his gaze away from Rod's piercing look. He was lying again, there was no doubt about that.

Rod nodded coldly. Speaking softly through his teeth, he said: 'I'm beginning to see now. You thought I was my brother, Hank Wellman.' He saw the man's head jerk upright at the mention of his brother's name, knew that he had hit the truth this time. He felt a tightness grow in him, as if steel bands had been placed around his chest and were being drawn tighter and tighter, threatening to shut off his breath. 'Could be that you know what happened to him, how he was killed.'

Ryan shook his head, but his hands were gripping the edge of the table tightly, knuckles standing out under the skin. His lips were thin, but whether with rage or fear it was difficult to tell. 'I don't know nothin' about your brother,' he said thickly. 'If he's dead, then I'm glad of it, but I didn't kill him, I —' He broke off sharply, his words ending in a bubbling moan as the gun in Rod's hand snaked forward, the foresight touching him on the cheek, raking across his skin, drawing blood. He pulled his head back with a sudden yell, one hand reaching up to touch his face. He stared down with a look of surprise on his features at the blood smeared on the back of his hand.

Eyes narrowed, breathing heavily, he half rose to his feet, hands clawed as though ready to grasp Rod around the throat and squeeze the life from him in spite of the gun levelled on him.

'Easy Ryan,' said the other man softly. His face was tight but there was a beat of sarcasm in his voice as he went on: 'We know nothing about your brother, friend, but we do know you and tomorrow, or the day after, we'll find you when you're not standing behind a gun. You may reckon you're tough, but you're not immune to a bullet or a knife.'

'You've had your chance to shoot me in the back,' Rod said tautly. He got slowly and deliberately to his feet, stood looking down at them. 'From now on, if I see either of your faces again, I'll use these guns and there won't be any chance for you then.'

Coolly, he walked out of the saloon, felt the doors close

behind him, touching his shoulders as he paused there for a second before stepping down into the street and untying the reins from the rail. Leading his horse around to the rear of the building, he found the hay bin, gave it plenty, then brought water to the trough. There were a handful of other horses there and it seemed that the bartender had been telling the truth when he said the livery stable was no longer in existence.

Satisfied that his horse had been cared for, he went back into the saloon. The card players were still there with the prospectors now losing steadily. A couple of men stood against the bar drinking. But there was no sign of the two gunslicks although the dishes were still on the table where they had been sitting a little while before. The bartender noticed the puzzled look on his face as he walked across to the bar.

Leaning over it, he said: 'They pulled out of here just after you left, Wellman. I guess they decided to take your advice and got out, unless they're waitin' somewhere out there in the darkness, waitin' to jump you the minute you show your face in the street again.'

Rod sighed. 'Then I reckon they'll have a long, cold wait. I'm goin' up to my room, if you'll show me where it is.'

'Sure, sure.' The other motioned him through a door in the bar, then along to the end, opening the door which led around towards the back of the building. There were a couple of steps leading up to a long corridor, with rooms on either side. All of the doors were closed and the other paused in front of the one at the far end, thrust the key into the lock, turned it, then stood to one side for Rod to enter.

There was little furniture inside the room. A low bed, a couple of chairs and a bureau near the window on which stood a jug and basin. But it was enough for a man who had been on the trail for so long and the sheets and blankets on the bed looked clean and inviting.

'Nothing like what you'd get over at the hotel, maybe,'

said the bartender apologetically, 'but I reckon it's reasonable at the price.'

'This will suit me fine,' Rod nodded. He walked to the window before lighting the lamp in the room, stood with his body pressed tightly against the wall, glancing out. The window looked down on one of the dark, unlit alleys he had noticed on his ride into Hatchet Bend. An excellent place for a man to move up to a window and shoot through it, he thought, but that was a risk he would have to take.

The bartender made to leave, but Rod stopped him at the door. 'You reckon you could give me some answers, friend?' he asked softly.

The other looked closely at him for a moment before replying. 'That depends on what it is you want to know,' he said with a touch of his earlier nervousness.

'You heard what that gunslick Ryan said. I reminded him of my brother. He would have shot me in the back for that. I know my brother's dead. I've got a telegram in my pocket to prove that. But I want to know how he died – and why? And, if possible, who killed him.'

'You won't find it easy to discover the answers to any of those questions. Your brother was Sheriff of Twin Ranchos. It's a town about forty miles from here to the north. All I know is that he took a posse out into the hills after a gang of outlaws led by a man called Matt Booth, smashed them and brought back most of them over the saddles of their horses. But Booth managed to get away during the gunfight.'

'How did my brother die?'

'I don't know. News gets changed on its way here. Some folk say one thing, and some another.'

'Then I reckon I'd better ride into Twin Ranchos and find out for myself.'

'If you're aimin' to ride in lookin' for vengeance, better watch your step. There are more killers in that town than any other place I know.' There was no doubting the seriousness and sincerity in the barkeep's voice. Rod eyed him closely for a moment, then nodded his head slowly.

'Thanks for the warning. I'll remember it.'

'Sure.' The other backed out into the corridor. He nodded his head towards a chair. 'The door has a lock but there have been times when it's been opened by some-body else. Better jam a chair under the handle. That way you'll get warning if anybody tries to get in through the night.'

'And the window?' Rod said tightly.

The bartender's gaze flickered momentarily towards the window, then he shrugged. 'Won't be easy to watch that. Looks out onto one of the alleys.'

'Guess I'll be asleep with my gun under the pillow just in case.' Rod closed the door after the other, turned the key in the lock, then placed the chair against it. He undressed in the dark, made little noise, splashed the cool water from the jug onto his face and head, felt the alkali mask crack as the water burned against his scorched skin where the sun had burned it during the long days across the desert.

Outside, the sky was clear, with the starlight casting a faint, shimmering glow over everything so that, now his eyes had grown accustomed to the darkness, he was able to make out details of the buildings around him. The alley was filled with piles of rubbish and debris in the shadows of which a man could find several hiding places. He thought for a moment of the two gunmen who had tried to shoot him in the back earlier that evening, in mistake for his brother, then put all thought of them from his mind.

Going back to the bed, he stretched himself out on it, placing one of the Colts under his pillow, his fingers still curled around the butt. As he lay there he turned things over in his mind, past events of the years since his brother had ridden away from the ranch, heading west. There had been little news of him during those long years, an occa-sional letter would arrive, posted in many towns scattered over the face of the great West. Apparently, Hank had worked at several jobs, cowpoke, trail-driver, once taking a wagon train through Indian country when nobody else would take on the job.

Rod felt a wave of gladness that his brother had been Sheriff of this town of Twin Ranchos when he had died. At least there had been nothing of which to be ashamed there. But there was the inescapable feeling in his mind that Hank had not been killed in fair fight and it was this thought which continued to rankle in his mind, giving him little rest, increasing the uneasiness, the restlessness in him. If Hank had been shot in cold blood, then he vowed he would find his killer and mete out the same sort of justice to him, but when the time came, he would make certain that the other knew who was killing him – and why.

At first light, he was awake and dressed, buckling the heavy gunbelt around his waist. He drank water from the pitcher and threw a swift, wary glance out of the window. The grey light of a nearly dawn was just beginning to wash over the town now. As yet, there was scarcely any colour in the sky or the drab buildings which he could see from the window. A new day was breaking for him, but Hank would no longer be able to see it, could no longer feel the wind on his face, or hear the steady abrasion of a horse's hooves in the dust of the street. It was as if a knife had been suddenly twisted inside him. Making his way into the saloon, he found both bartenders at work behind the bar, getting ready for the day. Things were slack at the moment and while his breakfast was being fried up for him, he went around the rear of the saloon, checked on his mount. There were only two other horses in sight and he recalled that there had been perhaps a dozen or so when he had brought the bay around the previous evening. Evidently, men went early about their work in this town. He fell to wondering what there was for them to do in a backwater such as Hatchet Bend, his forehead furrowed in deep thought as he turned the idea over in his mind.

Breakfast was ready for him when he went back inside.

A swamper brushed the floor, sweeping the debris of the previous night out into the street. The rustle of the brush was the only sound in the saloon as Rod sat down in his chair and ate the meal of bacon, eggs and sweet potatoes which was put down to him.

'See anythin' more of those two *hombres* after I went to bed?' he asked of the bartender.

The other shook his head. 'Guess they lit out of town,' he said softly.

'You got any idea where they work?'

'Heard they were running cattle for Jeff Carswell. He owns one of the big spreads between here and Twin Ranchos.'

'What sort of a character is he?'

The other shrugged. 'I've heard nothin' against him. There was a little talk a while ago of some rustlin'. They reckoned that his herd had grown mighty fast during the past few months, much faster than the normal calving could have accounted for.'

'Anybody bother to check on the brands?'

The man smiled thinly, meaningly. 'With a man as big as Carswell you don't check unless you're pretty sure and you can back up any accusation you want to make.'

'I get your meaning.' Rod swallowed the hot coffee. It burned his throat, but he forced it down, felt better for it. 'He hires men like those two gunhawks to make sure that nobody dares to make any accusation against him.'

'That's right. So far, anybody who has tried, didn't live long.'

'You reckon he might have had anythin' to do with my brother's death?'

'Could be. I wouldn't like to say anythin' about that. Maybe if he thought your brother had found any real evidence against him of rustlin', he might have given orders to stop him for good. Carswell didn't get where he is now by taking any risks at all.'

Rod was silent, thinking about that. There seemed to be a lot of loose ends lying around with nothing to help him tie them together. There was little more that the bartender could tell him and Rod knew better than to rely on hearsay evidence which would obviously have been coloured and exaggerated after being passed by word of mouth for so long.

He rode out of Hatchet Bend just as the sun was coming up redly over the eastern horizon. The trail grew rougher as he progressed, leading him up into the foothills and although he cast about him for any way down through the valley it was soon obvious to him that he would lose time trying to ride in that direction. Putting his horse up into the rocky passes, he climbed higher among the upjutting crags that lifted in twisted pinnacles on either side of him.

The sun lifted, grew stronger and little beads of sweat formed on his neck and face. The road up through the hills was a narrow streak of dust, in places almost obliterated by the last rain to have fallen. As he rode, he fell wondering whether or not there might be a stage road connecting Hatchet Bend with Twin Ranchos. There would have been at one time or another, since in those booming days of ten years earlier, the stage road would be needed to transport the wagon trains and coaches taking gold back east and supplies out to this area. Funny he had seen no sign of it during the ride out of Hatchet Bend. Could be, he mused, that it had become overgrown during the years when it had not been used and he had missed it.

He was ten miles up into the hills and it was almost noon, before the trail levelled, then dipped downgrade in front of him. A swift-running stream had worn a narrow fissure in the rock across the trail and he rode through it the water foaming around his horse's feet. Pausing on the far bank to let the animal blow and drink, he thought he made out the tag-end of criss-crossing sounds in the deeper silence of the hills, but he could not be certain. There was no dust in the air to indicate the presence of other men riding this trail but he knew nothing of other trails which might be present higher up the craggy slopes.

Mounting up once more, he rode on, moving down towards the valley which he guessed lay at the foot of the hills. His horse frequently slowed now, knowing its own mind and he did not bother to urge it on. Now that the trail was almost at its end and he knew he would reach Twin Ranchos by nightfall, a little of the urgency in his mind was fading. But as he rode, he watched the grey-black foreground of rock and thin earth more closely. If the stories he had heard of this part of the territory were true, then gold had been found in these hills and others around Twin Ranchos, contributing in large part to the increased prosperity of the town, lifting it from its former status as a ghost-town with only a handful of inhabitants, to a brawling, booming town, the saloons and gambling halls coming to life once more, run by men equally as ruthless and deadly as the others who had built them.

The emptiness of the hills seemed a signal of danger to come, something to heed. He looked anxiously to the shadowed banks of rock on either side of him as he rode forward into a steep-sided canyon, the floor littered with huge boulders which had, at some time in the distant past, been torn from the rocky faces and fallen to the bottom. Carefully, his mount picked its way around them. The canyon was a deep fissure in the rocks, perhaps a quarter of a mile in length and he was glad when he saw the walls begin to taper downward, broadening his view of the terrain around him.

He had scarcely passed out into the bright sunlight again when a rifle shot blasted from the rocks to his left and Rod felt the whipping sting of the bullet as it plucked at the sleeve of his jacket, laying a red weal across his left arm.

Yanking the Winchester from its boot, he dropped like a stone from the saddle, hit the ground hard, pulling on the reins with his free hand as he did so, so that the horse was between him and the drygulcher. He struck the rocks with his shoulder and for a moment, a numbing agony lanced along his arms, almost causing him to release his hold on the rifle. Rolling instinctively, he came over onto his stomach behind one of the boulders, heard a second shot, followed by the thin scream of the bullet as it chipped stone from the top of the boulder and ricocheted off along the canyon. Another hastily aimed bullet struck dirt a couple of feet from where he lay and he swore harshly under his breath as he realized that he had ridden blindly into an ambush. Those sounds he had heard near the stream should have warned him of trouble; voices being carried along above the water. Probably at that time, the man, or men, for such he guessed them to be, were a mile or so along the stream, watching him as he rode the trail below them. Had his mind been alert, he would have guessed that an ambush might have been set up for him. Deep inside him, he had no doubt who it was, crouched among those rocks up there. Ryan and that sidekick of his, out to kill him for what had happened in the saloon the previous evening. He grimaced as he lifted his head cautiously, an inch at a time, risking a quick look around him. Where he was lying, the shadow of the rocks at his back threw a dark shadow over the ground and he realized with a faint sense of relief that he would be able to pick out any slight movement up there in the rocks which were flooded by the brilliant sunlight, whereas it would be more difficult for either of those two killers to spot him in the dimness.

It occurred to him that there might be something more to this ambush than just revenge on the part of those two bushwhackers. They would have had plenty of time during the night to have ridden back to the Carswell ranch and informed Jeff Carswell of his presence in Hatchet Bend. If Carswell was implicated in Hank's murder, then he would undoubtedly have given them the order to kill him before he could make any trouble. The rancher would not want him to get into Twin Ranchos alive if he was in any way the cause of Hank's death.

Squinting up against the glaring sunlight, reflected

from the smooth rocks which overlooked the trail at this point, he realized that the drygulchers had chosen the place for their ambush well and evidently they knew this area equally well. They would be able to watch every inch of the trail out of the canyon, and would also be able to make sure that he had no chance to backtrail into it. They were sure to get him if they could keep him pinned down there long enough. It only needed one of them to remain perched high among the rocks to keep him there, while the other circled around to the other side of the trail and came up behind him. He glanced quickly over his shoulder, peering up at the wall of the canyon. Here, where it petered out slowly, it was less than ten feet high. A man could easily scale it and shoot down on him from the rocky ledge at his back. Sucking in a harsh gust of air, he assessed the situation. He had to make a move before these men got around to trying to attack him from the rear. Pulling his hat from his head, he lifted it cautiously around the edge of the boulder. Almost at once, there came another blasting roar and the hat was plucked from the end of the rifle and spun several yards away, a neat round hole in the crown.

Nearby his horse whinnied softly at the sound of the gunshot. It began to edge away from him, moving out of the canyon. Glancing quickly to his right, he noticed the line of boulders which stretched for perhaps twenty yards along the edge of the trail. A distance of six or seven feet separated him from the nearest but if the horse continued to edge in that direction, he might be able to make a dash for it, keeping behind the cover of his mount. It was his only chance and easing himself upright a little, he got his legs under him, ready to leap out the moment his opportunity came.

Another shot came, this time some distance further along the trail and he grinned tightly to himself as he heard it. That would be the other man, firing in his direction. He reckoned the man was about thirty yards further along the trail, was probably going to try to get across it and pin him down, boxing him in against the canyon wall.

The horse was now halfway between himself and the line of boulders and he suddenly launched himself forward, threw himself flat across the last couple of feet, scrabbling forward as gunshots blasted the silence. Dust spurted where the bullets struck. Clawing desperately with outstretched hands, he hauled himself, gasping hoarsely with the effort, into the shelter of the rocks, moved quickly and without pause to the far end. He guessed the dry-gulchers would be expecting him to remain where he was, at the nearer end of the string of boulders until he got his breath back and assessed the position and they would be concentrating most of their attention there instead of watching for him at the other end.

Swiftly, he settled himself down on the hard, stony ground, glanced around the edge of the boulder. There was a sudden movement some thirty feet from him, among the rocks. He caught a fragmentary glimpse of a figure scrambling down towards the trail. Sunlight flashed bluely on the barrel of the rifle in the man's hands. In the glare, he could not recognize the other, but he knew the man was taking advantage of his previous move to get across the trail.

Swiftly, he jerked up the rifle, laid the barrel across the low rocks in front of him, caught the other in the sights, and squeezed the trigger. The Winchester recoiled against his wrists and over the sights he saw the drygulcher stagger as he made to jump down onto the trail. For a long moment the other remained upright, his head turned, a look of astonishment imprinted on it. Then the muscles of his jaw and cheeks loosened, the rifle dropped from his slowly opening fingers, and he flopped forward onto his knees, struck the edge of the rock, fell onto the trail some four feet below him, bounced once or twice, then lay still, arms flung out in front of him, legs twisted at a curious angle under his body.

The slowly atrophying echoes of the show died away among the rocks. In the deep silence that followed, he listened desperately for any movement which would give away the position of the other man. Wherever he was, he must have seen what had happened to his companion, would know that the odds had been evened now and that he was in danger.

The silence lengthened, grew more intense. Rod lay absolutely still, every nerve strained. The other man was making no move now. Perhaps he was too shaken by the sudden and unexpected turn of events. Perhaps he realized that the tables had now been turned with a vengeance and instead of being the hunter, he might now have become the hunted.

Several minutes dragged by without any movement from the remaining drygulcher. Rod knew he was up there somewhere, maybe waiting for him to make the first move, hoping he would make a mistake and give himself away. He smiled grimly to himself. He did not intend to throw away his life now. He had taken on the two of them and now one lay dead in the dust of the trail and the other man had been suddenly thrown onto the defensive. He meant to keep it that way, knowing that his own patience could make stone of him until the other man broke under the growing strain.

At last, he heard the sudden scrape of boots on the rock. It came from a little to one side of him, high up among the ragged boulders. He turned his head sharply at the faint sound, knowing he had not been mistaken. A loose stone came rattling down the steep side of the canyon wall and struck the rocky floor a couple of yards from where he lay. The other was getting restless, he thought tautly. Maybe he was trying to figure out a way of getting back to his mount and riding on out of there while he still had a whole skin.

Reaching up slowly with his left hand, he wiped the sweat from his face, blinked his eyes against the harsh glare, let his gaze wander slowly from side to side. Suddenly, the other broke. The lone minutes of strain and silence had proved too much for him. He began firing recklessly down into the boulders, hoping to hit Rod provided he fired enough shots. Rod kept his head low, listened to the bullets singing around him, some cutting into the dust, others ricocheting from one wall of the canyon to the other as they fled along it.

For a long moment, the man remained hidden, with probably only the barrel of his rifle thrust through a cleft in the rocks. Then there came the sound of boots on rock as he turned and ran, retreating back into the crags heading for his mount. Rod raised himself up onto his knees to get a shot at the fleeing gunman, but the other only showed himself at brief intervals as he ran from one rocky ledge to another, moving further and further into the hills. He caught a brief glimpse of the other as he ran across an open stretch of ground, whipped up the rifle and fired, but knew from the way the man ran on that the shot had missed. A few seconds later, there was the sound of a horse being ridden away at a reckless pace, the steady abrasion of hoofbeats fading swiftly into the distance as the man made off. There was probably an old Indian trail up there, Rod guessed, and knew that he had very little chance of catching up with the other now. By the time he managed to get his horse up there to that trail, the man would be miles away, beyond his reach.

He went forward to where the dead man lay in the middle of the trail, bent beside him, turning him over. It was the young man he had seen with Ryan the previous evening. There was a red stain on his shirt, just left of the breastbone and he must have died almost instantly. Straightening up, Rod went back to his horse, thrust the Winchester back into the boot. Tightening the cinch, he mounted up, sat the saddle for a moment, looking about him. The smell of powder still hung in the air and there was a faint, drifting haze in the sunlight.

At least, he now had a pretty good idea who that other man had been. It could have been none other than Ryan and he knew that sooner or later, he would meet up with the other again and force a showdown.

By the time he was out of the hills, riding through more open country, the sun had passed its zenith and was westering slowly, but the heat had continued to rise in intensity and the metal of the bridle sent painful flashes of light into his eyes as he rode.

Gradually, the country around him changed. He rode out of the broad valley, crossed a sluggishly-flowing river, then entered a land of sand and clay, with narrow gulches that split the earth, now filled with shadow as the sun went down. A few trees lifted from the clayey soil, short and stunted and there were large areas of thorn through which he was forced to pick his way carefully. Ahead of him lay the benchlands where he guessed Twin Ranchos lay. Passing through timber an hour later, with the piney smell of the trees in his nostrils and the cool greenness around him, he began to feel a little of the taut apprehension boil up inside him. If those two killers in Hatchet Bend had recognized him as kin to Hank, then it was more than likely the same would happen in Twin Ranchos and he could expect trouble. The horse increased its pace as they came out of the timber, moving downgrade a little. The sun had sunk below the undulating line of hills far to the west and only the up-spreading red rays were touching the sky. A few clouds shone crimson as the sunlight touched them, but everything else on the earth was in deep shadow, blue and still, with the cool wind blowing off the distant hills, flowing against his face.

His shadow lay long at his back and in front of him, the dusk was a water-blue colour, still and deep. The hills were black and high, bulky in places and in others formed into slender spires of rock. Directly ahead of him lay Twin Ranchos. In the dusk, he could make out the main street which was the trail on which he had been riding, widening as it ran through the town, out on the other side, leading up towards the hills.

The town was larger than he had imagined, with double rows of single-storey houses on both sides of the street near the edge of the place, broadening out with taller buildings and warehouses in the centre. Another trail, slanting in from the north, joined the main street halfway along it, forming a junction.

He found the livery stables, led his horse into the darkened rear and handed it over to the man who drifted towards him from the shadows, with only the red, glowing tip of the cigarette in his mouth, lighting his gaunt features, the flesh laid close to the high cheek bones. Rod watched the old fellow, wondered how much this man might know of what went on in town. It was possible he knew more than he would tell. These men saw a lot but talked little, knowing that it was not healthy to tell of what they saw. A man who kept silent, had a far better chance of staying alive in a town like this, than one who went around shooting off his mouth.

Moving out onto the boardwalk, he paused with his back against one of the wooden uprights, rolled a cigarette and lit it. The groom stood beside him, watching him from bright beady eyes and as Rod turned his head, the orange flare of the match still lighting his features, he heard the other's sharp intake of breath. The man muttered something under his breath and took a sudden step backward.

'Somethin' worrying you friend?' Rod asked mildly.

'Why, no – nothin',' murmured the other. He pulled himself together with a visible effort. 'It's just that you —'

'That I remind you of somebody else.' Rod grinned down at him, but there was no mirth in the smile and it did not touch his eyes. 'Hank Wellman, perhaps?'

The man said nothing for a long moment but continued to stare at him fixedly. Then he said huskily. 'There is a likeness, mister. But you —'

'I'm his brother,' Rod said flatly. 'I got word he'd been killed here and I aim to find out how. Maybe you could tell me somethin' about it.'

The groom shook his head tightly. He smoked nervously on his cigarette, his hands trembling a little. 'I don't know a thing, mister.' He spoke hopefully as though wanting Rod to believe him.

'Anybody in town who might know somethin'?'

'You could ask Kerby. He's the mayor and I reckon if anybody was to know, he'd be the man.'

'Anybody else?'

The oldster pursed his lips. 'You might try Charlie Ferris. He's the deputy. He was the man who found your brother.'

'Where will I find him?'

'If he ain't in the Sheriff's office, you'll find him in one of the saloons. Guess he's your best man.'

'Ferris.' Rod nodded, dropped the butt of his cigarette onto the dusty street and ground it out with his heel. 'Thanks.' He tossed a coin to the other, then made his way along the street. He found the Sheriff's office a couple of blocks along. There was a yellow light showing through the dusty window, spilling out onto the boardwalk and he guessed that Ferris was in. Climbing the wooden steps onto the boardwalk, he lifted his hand to rap on the door, then paused as loud voices from inside reached him.

A harsh voice said tightly: 'You know as well as I do Ferris, that there's nothin' we can do about this. We've got the orders and we have to carry them out. If you want to start questioning them, that's your business. But when I'm told to see to it that he doesn't stick around this place, then I mean to see that he doesn't. You know what happened the last time.'

'I still don't like it,' said another voice, worried, low. 'Sooner or later, somebody is goin' to cotton' on to what's happening and then this whole town is goin' to blow up in our faces. Have you ever thought of that?'

'Everythin' will be taken care of. Besides, you're gettin' your cut, aren't you? What more do you want?'

'I want to make sure I stay alive to enjoy it,' snapped the other man. 'Things are coming to a head and —'

Rod rapped loudly on the door. There was a long silence in the office, then he heard a voice yell. 'Who is it?'

In answer, Rod opened the door and stepped inside. The man seated behind the desk, with his legs propped on top of it, was thin-faced, his wide-brimmed hat tilted back on his head. He swung his legs to the floor as Rod walked in, the yellow light of the lamp on the desk falling dull on his face. Both men in the room stared at him, with their mouths dropping slackly open. Then the man with the deputy's star pinned on his shirt managed to regain control of himself. He closed his mouth with an audible snap, said thinly: 'Who are you, mister?'

'The name's Wellman – Rod Wellman,' he said quietly, noticing the reaction which his words produced.

'Wellman!' Ferris stared at the man seated opposite him. He swallowed thickly and then forced a smile onto his lips. 'You related to Hank Wellman?'

'That's right. He was my brother. I got a message saying he had been killed here and I came along to find out how – and by whom.'

The other man rose heavily to his feet. He stood for a moment eyeing Rod curiously, then he said with a deceptive mildness: 'I wouldn't go poking your nose into too many things here in Twin Ranchos,' he said, his tone growing harsher. 'There are a lot of people around who might not like it.'

'Oh?' Rod raised his brows slightly. 'You tryin' to warn me there might be trouble?'

'That's right,' nodded the other. He brushed past Rod and moved towards the door. Over his shoulder, he said to Ferris. 'Better remember what I said earlier, Charlie. Unless you want trouble – big trouble.'

THREE
Outlaw Valley

'Seems to me that he's got somethin' on his mind,' Rod said casually, as he lowered himself into the seat which the other had just vacated. He eyed Ferris closely across the desk, could see that the other man was ill at ease, and that his presence had seemed to heighten the tension in the other's mind. Ferris fidgeted with the papers on the desk, brows drawn together into a single line.

'You came ridin' into Twin Ranchos looking for trouble, Wellman?' he said finally, and it was more of a statement than a question. 'I don't like that. This is a bad town at any time. Your brother was Sheriff here and he had his work cut out tryin' to clean it up. Somehow, I doubt if anybody can do that. There are some towns that can be tamed, and others that can't – and this is one of them.'

'Depends on who does the tamin',' Rod said significantly. He recalled some of the conversation which he had overheard standing outside the door and he could tell from the look in the deputy's eyes and the twist of the man's lips that the same thought had struck him, and Ferris was wondering just how much he had heard before he had knocked on the door.

Ferris forced himself to relax, sitting back in his chair. He placed his hands flat on the desk in front of him, said with a tense quietness: 'I can understand your feelings. You don't know how your brother died and you want to find out to set things straight in your mind.'

Rod nodded. 'That's part of it,' he agreed, noticing the tight set of the other's mouth. 'The groom at the livery stables said that you were the man who found him, that you could tell me what happened.'

Ferris sighed audibly. 'I can tell you very little. Sure, I found him the next morning. He'd been shot down sometime through the night. His room was on the ground floor of the hotel, at the side of the building. Somebody must have got to him during the night, smashed the window and fired at him as he lay in bed.'

'You say you found him in the morning. Did nobody hear the shot that killed him?'

'Obviously not.' Ferris looked distinctly unhappy. 'Don't ask me why. Either there's somebody lyin', or nobody was around when he was killed. Either way, I couldn't get anybody to talk.'

'And you've no idea who could have done it?'

'Sure, I've got ideas. But I can't do anythin' without proof. You know that, Wellman. Much as I hate to be beat, I can't arrest anybody for murder unless I can prove they did it. You've got to understand this town to know how difficult it is. Your brother had taken out a posse a few days before he died, to hunt down a man called Matt Booth, a wanted outlaw who had shot up the town and robbed the bank here. They cornered him in the hills, killed most of the men he had with him. But Booth managed to get away. Maybe he didn't ride out as far as we thought. Maybe he made his way back into town after dark, determined to take his revenge on your brother. He could have shot him down and ridden out again.'

Tight-lipped, Rod listened to the other nodding his head slowly. That made some kind of sense he was forced to admit. He could see now why Ferris had been unable to make an arrest. If it had been this killer Booth the man would have reached the border sometime the following day and there would be no way of getting him. On the other hand this theory that Booth had been responsible for Hank's death was purely conjecture on Ferris's part. There were undoubtedly others in Twin Ranchos and the surrounding territory who might want Hank dead.

'You know anythin' of a man called Ryan?' he asked abruptly leaning forward.

Ferris looked startled by the question then veiled the look in his eyes swiftly. 'Ryan?' He seemed to turn the name over in his mind. 'The name is familiar.' Then he nodded. 'Sure he's the foreman at the Lazy Y ranch, Jeff Carswell's spread.'

'What do you know of him?'

'Only that he's a fast man with a gun. He usually keeps out of Twin Ranchos, so we have little to do with him. But he's a dangerous man to cross. They say he's killed several men in fair fight.'

'You surprise me,' murmured Rod dryly. 'He tried to shoot me in the back in the saloon in Hatchet Bend yesterday and tried to drygulch me with a friend of his on the way here today. The man with him is dead, but Ryan managed to get away into the hills.'

Ferris narrowed his eyes at the news. He seemed to regard Rod with a new respect. 'Why should they want to try to kill you?'

'Could be that they knew who I was and guessed why I'm here. You know if Hank had anythin' on Carswell?'

'Carswell?' There was genuine surprise in the deputy's voice. He shook his head slowly. 'I'm sure he didn't. Certainly he never mentioned anythin' to me about him. He's a big man in these parts with plenty of influence.'

'I've heard that for myself. But they reckon that he only had a small herd when he arrived in this neck of the woods and that quite suddenly, he seemed to become extremely prosperous. Now what does that suggest to you?'

'Nothing much,' muttered the other. He got to his feet, stood looking down at Rod for a moment with an expression of perplexity on his narrow features. 'I could say that whatever Carswell has done is no concern of yours, or mine, unless he breaks the law. Maybe he had a couple of good years with the calving. It's happened before.'

'There's a quicker and surer way of building up a herd,' Rod reminded the other. 'And in Hatchet Bend, that's the way they seem to think he did it. There were several smaller ranchers who lost a lot of cattle around that time apparently. Rustlin' ain't difficult, if you've got yourself a good bunch of men, handy with a gun.'

'You sayin' that Carswell rustled those cattle of his?' Ferris tightened his lips into a thin line. 'Unless you can prove a thing like that, I'd better warn you against saying it. If it gets to Carswell's ears, you could find yourself in big trouble.'

Rod grinned tightly. Pushing back his chair, he stood up, faced the other. 'Seems to me I've heard those very same words a few minutes ago. Just what sort of trouble would you be in, Ferris?'

A dark wave of colour suffused the deputy's face. His fingers gripped the edge of the desk with a convulsive tightness. Then he forced himself to relax. 'That has nothin' to do with you, mister,' he said thickly. 'I'm the law in this town and I'm warnin' you to watch your step so long as you stay here. I'm sorry about what happened to your brother, but he ain't the first Sheriff to get himself shot in the line of duty, and I don't suppose he'll be the last. But remember this. Don't start getting any fancy ideas about snooping around town, askin' a lot of fool questions, trying to find out who shot your brother. If you do that, you're likely to wind up here in jail, if you don't wind up dead in some alley first. I don't want trouble in town. I've got enough on my plate right now. So keep that gun in its holster whenever you're around.'

'I ain't here to make trouble, Ferris,' Rod said calmly. He faced the other man down. 'But if I do find out who shot Hank down like that, I'll not stop until he's dead.' His lips thinned into a grin. 'In the meantime, better watch your own troubles, Ferris.'

With this parting shot, he opened the door and stepped out into the street. In the hotel, halfway along the street, he signed his name in the register, asked for a bath and was surprised to find that he could get one. It seemed that Twin Ranchos was well on the way back to its former glory, he thought, so he let the hot water soak all of the stiffness from his bones, loosening the muscles, bringing a sense of well-being back into his tired body.

He ate his evening meal in the dining room on the ground floor, ignoring the looks given him by the sleepy clerk in the lobby or the other diners. When he had finished, he walked across the street to one of the saloons, laid his elbows on the bar and rested his weight on them. There was a poker game running at one of the tables and most of the men in the saloon were either playing or gathered around, watching the game.

Finishing his drink, he went out again, stood for a while in the shadows and then went over to the hotel. The town seemed quiet, but that could be a surface thing and judging from what he had heard through the door of the Sheriff's office, things could blow up in their faces at any moment. He wondered what orders those men had been given and which Ferris had not wanted to carry out.

Collecting his key from the clerk, he went along to his room, up the creaking stairs and along the short corridor at the top. The key rattled in the lock, then he thrust the door open and stopped instantly. The room beyond lay in darkness, seemed just as he had left it, yet there was an overpowering feeling that the room was no longer empty, that there was someone there, hiding in the shadows, waiting for him to step through the door. Carefully, he lifted one of the Colts from its holster, hefted it into his right hand, finger straight on the trigger, thumb just touching the top of the hammer, ready to jerk it back and let it go at a moment's notice.

Then he kicked the door open sharply so that the light from the corridor spilled inside, touching the objects there with a pale glow. The door crashed back against the wall as he darted swiftly to one side and he knew there was no one waiting just there to hit him over the head the minute he moved inside. Swiftly, he peered about him, his body in a half crouched stance as he tried to make out whoever it was.

There was a sudden, almost startled movement at the far side of the room and a slight figure rose from the chair and turned hurriedly to face him. He had a brief glimpse of a white dress and long, burnished hair that shone faintly in the dim light, then he lowered the gun a little foolishly, closed the door behind him, and walked forward in the darkness.

Finding a match, he struck it and lit the lamp on the small table. The bright yellow glow spread swiftly throughout the room and he looked up to find the girl watching him with wide eyes, her lips parted a little, one hand on the back of the chair as though to steady herself.

'Mister Wellman?' she said in a soft, rich voice.

He nodded, a puzzled look on his face. 'That is my name,' he said quietly. 'But I'm afraid I don't understand. How did you get into my room, and what are you doing here anyway?'

'The clerk is a particular friend of mine,' she explained, sitting down again. She motioned to the other chair by the window and he noticed that she had taken the precaution of closing the wooden shutters. 'My name is Julie Saunders. Your brother once did my father a very great service. If it hadn't been for him, Carswell would have taken us over completely, would have run his herd onto our grazing land making it impossible for us to feed our own cattle.'

'But that still doesn't explain why you're here and at this time of the night.'

'This is a hell town,' explained the girl. She spoke quite frankly and bluntly. 'There are more killers here than in any other town I know and it won't be long before they set up something for you as they did for Hank.'

Rod eyed her steadily for a long moment. 'What do you

know about Hank's death?' he asked. In spite of himself, his voice seemed tight and brutal.

'Very little. I know that he made a lot of enemies here. But he was a straight man, honest, determined to uphold the law and that didn't sit too well with a lot of the others. He couldn't be bought and that rankled with Carswell and when he threatened to bring him in and jail him for contempt if he didn't get those cattle of his off our land, Carswell swore that he'd finish him.'

'Do you know that for a fact, or is it just hearsay like so many of the other things I've been hearing?'

The girl smiled faintly. 'I know it for a fact, Mister Wellman. I was there when Carswell made the threat. It was shortly after that, he started bringing in killers from near the border. He reckoned they were driving up some cattle for him from Texas, but when they got here it was soon plain what sort of men they were and why he'd hired them.'

'I may have already met up with two of them,' Rod said grimly. He related what had happened to him on the way there, at Hatchet Bend and along the trail.

She listened intently until he had finished, then nodded her head slowly. 'Now you know what I mean. Somebody set it up for your brother and if you're not careful they will do the same for you.' She looked at him, her troubled mind seeming to relax a little. 'There are few men in this town you will be able to trust. Have you spoken with Charlie Ferris yet?'

Rod nodded. 'I went to see him as soon as I got into town. The groom at the livery stable said he might be the only person who could help me find the answers to some of the questions I need to have answered.'

'Don't trust him. Even though he is the deputy Sheriff now, he's working with Carswell. I'm sure of it.'

Rod debated whether to tell her what he had heard through the door of the other's office, but decided against it. He knew little of this girl as yet, and his suspicious mind was still tickled by the feeling that there were people here in town who seemed to know more about every move he made, than he liked. It was just possible that they were using the girl as bait to find out more about what he knew, and what he intended to do.

'I can understand you not likin' Carswell, but so far there seems to be no real evidence against him.'

'Perhaps if you were to look around a little you might find some, maybe even something to link him with your brother's death.'

Rod eyed her in mild surprise. There was a certain hardness in her tone that did not go with the innocent expression on her face. He studied her over a long thoughtful interval. Her shoulders were brown from long exposure to the sun and there was a directness to her glance which he felt oddly disconcerting. He was surprised at her cold, rational analysis of him, but guessed there was something more at the back of her statements than he guessed at the moment.

'You want me to implicate Carswell and then kill him?'

'Yes,' she said.

'I know how you feel, but I sure hate to hear hardness in a woman. What happened between you and Carswell has hit you hard and there may be somethin' in what you say, but I need proof first before I go gunnin' for any man.'

'How much more proof do you want? His two hired hands ambushed you on the trail here, did their best to kill you.'

He said, half-angrily. 'I know that. But they could have tried that out on their own account without Carswell either giving them any orders or even knowing about it.'

She swung about, facing him, her will as strong as his. She flung her question at him. 'Why would they pick on you? The only thing that picks you out from a crowd is your resemblance to your brother.'

Rod was silent at that, remembering what Ryan had said when he had first seen him, knew there was a lot of truth in what the girl had said. He sighed, stood by the window, watching her closely, trying to make up his mind about her, what she really wanted from him. Revenge for what Carswell had done? It seemed likely. He gave her a strange look. 'I'll keep my eyes and ears open around town,' he promised. 'Believe me, I want to find out what happened to Hank and when I do, I won't rest until I've hunted down his killer, no matter where he is.'

'I see.' She sounded disappointed as she moved towards the door. The stiffness on her face was clearly visible, the set of her lips, full yet compressed a little as they lay together. She was, he guessed, a woman with a will of her own, not used to being denied anything she had set her mind upon. In the doorway, she paused. 'If you ever need any kind of help, ride out to the Triple Star ranch. I'll do everything I can.'

Rod gave a slight nod. He saw her smiling at him faintly, guessed that she believed she had made him see things her way. She had a great deal of pride, he thought after she had gone and a burning, all-consuming hatred for Carswell. Maybe the rancher had played a part in Hank's death; that was something he would have to find out.

'So you're Hank Wellman's brother,' Mayor Kerby murmured. He sat in the chair near the window and eyed Rod closely, very little emotion on his flabby features. 'I figured if he had any kin at all, they might be payin' us a visit someday, but I didn't expect you here so soon. How did you get to know that he'd been killed?'

'This,' Rod said. 'I got it a couple of weeks ago.' He pulled the telegram form from his pocket and held it out to the other.

Kerby took it and perused it carefully for several moments before handing it back. 'I see it was sent off from here,' he said thoughtfully. 'But there's no signature here to say who sent it.'

'That's what had me wonderin',' Rod admitted. 'I figured it might have been a hoax at first, but I decided to head in this direction and find out. Seems it was no hoax.'

Kerby nodded his head ponderously in agreement. 'I only wish it was,' he said harshly. 'I'm mighty sorry about what happened to your brother. He made us a real fine Sheriff. In a way, I feel responsible for what happened to him.'

'How was that?' Rod gave him a bright-sharp stare. Kerby spread his hands in a meaningful gesture. 'I came to see him shortly after he'd ridden back into town with the bodies of the outlaws they killed up in the hills. I told him that Booth, the man who led those murderin' thieves, would keep on ridin' once his band had been smashed, and that there would be nothin' whatever for us to fear from him again, certainly not until he had somehow managed to gather more men around him, when it was just possible he might come ridin' back seeking vengeance.' He sighed expansively. 'It seems I must've been wrong. Maybe if I'd only had the sense to realize that as far as men such as Booth are concerned, vengeance is the one thing uppermost in their minds, that they think of nothin' but destroying a man who has bested them, your brother would have been alerted to his danger.'

'Then the way you figure it, is that this *hombre* Booth came back into town that night, sneaked into the alley near the hotel and fired that shot into Hank's room?'

Kerby lifted his head sharply. His eyes held a bright look. 'Don't you?' he asked tautly. 'Surely there's no doubt at all about it. Nobody else would have shot him down like that. Nobody else had any motive. I know there were some folk in town who didn't like him overmuch. The men who run the gambling saloons were against him from the start because he refused to accept their bribes and warned them that if they stepped out of line, he'd see to it that the law was carried out. But in general, unless there was any real trouble, he turned a blind eye to some of their activities. No – I'm sure it was Booth. That sidewinder must've slunk back into town after dark and killed your brother.'

'I've been hearing other things since I got here,' said Rod quietly, his cold, expressionless eyes watching the Mayor.

'Other things?' Kerby lifted his massive weight restlessly in his chair. His thick brows lifted into an interrogative line.

'There are folk here who think that maybe Jeff Carswell had a hand in Hank's murder.'

'Carswell.' For a moment there was a tiny flicker of emotion at the back of the other's deep-set eyes, then it was gone. His face remained motionless. He pushed himself back in his chair, licked his lips, then shook his head vehemently. 'I wouldn't set any store by that, mister. Carswell is a mighty big man in these parts and maybe some of the things he's done in the past to get where he is, weren't on the right side of the law. But there was no reason for him to be mixed up in somethin' like this. Surely you're not goin' to believe that talk?'

'Let's say I'm keeping an open mind until I find out somethin' definite. When I do, then I intend to do somethin' about it.'

Kerby studied the face of the cold-eyed man seated in front of him, looked for some trace of emotion there, but found none. He said slowly. 'I can tell by the look on your face that you've found no peace anywhere on the trail since you got that telegram and you'll find none here in Twin Ranchos. You'll always have to use a smoking six-gun, watch for men ready to shoot you in the back at the first chance they get. What sort of a life is that going to be for you, even if you manage to live through it?'

'Could be that you've got me wrong, Mayor,' said Rod dryly. 'It might be that the only thing I have to live for now is to avenge my brother's death. You say that he was Sheriff of this town and the way you figure it is that he was killed in the line of duty. Then why hasn't somethin' been done to try to find his killer and bring him to justice? You've got yourself a deputy Sheriff. He could have tried to do something.'

Kerby shrugged. 'It seemed so obvious to us that it was Booth who killed him that we never started to look anyplace else. And knowing Booth, once he'd done what he set out to do, he'd ride on out and keep on riding until he was well across the border where we'd never find him.'

'He stayed around once. He might be doing the same now, figuring that's the way you would all think. Seems to me he could still be around here someplace. Up there in the hills, there's gold in plenty and it would take a lot to keep him from that. Besides, those hills probably harbour more rustlers, killers and outlaws than any other place in this territory. He'll find all the men he wants there.'

'Could be that you're right,' agreed the other. 'But it would be sheer suicide to try to take a posse out into those hills looking for a man like Booth. There are too many trails there and those hills stretch for close on a hundred miles, are about fifty miles across. Plenty of places for a man to hide from the law.'

Rod drew his brows together thoughtfully. He was recalling that fragment of conversation he had heard outside the Sheriff's office the previous night. It was beginning to make a little sense now, enough sense to make him say softly: 'I figure it might be easier to find Booth than you seem to think, Kerby. I've got myself an idea that there might be somebody around town who can lead me right to him.'

Kerby looked startled for a moment at that statement, seemed on the point of saying something in reply, leaning forward with his hands gripping the sides of the chair. Then he sank slowly back and continued to stare straight at the other, lips pressed into a tight line across his puffy features. Then he said: 'I can't stop you in this venture of yours, and remembering what happened to Hank, I don't think I want to. But I'll have to give you this one warning. Don't try to step outside of the law, whatever you do, otherwise I'll have to see to it that Ferris brings you in. The fact that you're Hank's brother can't be allowed to stand in the way of justice.'

Nodding, Rod got to his feet, went out into the street, climbed up into the saddle and pulled his mount out into the middle of the road. As yet, the idea in his mind was only half-formed and he was not sure whether or not he had been right in his assumption. The man he wanted to see was the ferret-faced man who had been in the Sheriff's office, deep in heated conversation with Ferris when he had gone across there the evening before. Maybe the man did not look as though he would scare easily, but there were big things at stake here and Rod knew he would not hesitate to do anything to make the other tell him what he wanted to know.

But how to find that man? He had seen him only for those few brief moments before the other had sidled out of the door. He could have been another of Jeff Carswell's hands and if that was the case, it would not be easy to get to him, unlesss he rode in at night for a drink and a game of poker.

Across the street, he saw Ferris step out of his office on to the boardwalk, pause with his back against one of the uprights, lighting a smoke. The lawman was watching him closely over the cigarette even though he was trying to make himself seem casual. Rod reined up as the other stepped down into the street and moved out a little ahead of him.

'Been lookin' for you, Wellman,' said Ferris harshly. He squinted up at Rod.

The other shrugged. 'So you've found me,' he said quietly. 'What's on your mind?'

'Just want to make sure you don't go off half-cock in town. Be careful who you mix with around these parts. It's awful easy to get with the wrong crowd.'

'I don't recollect ever sayin' I intended to mix with anybody,' Rod said pointedly. 'Another thing; everybody seems to be intent on warning me against startin' any trouble. You'd think some of 'em might have somethin' to hide the way they go on.'

Ferris narrowed his eyes. For a moment a sharp retort lay on his lips, then he obviously thought better of it, said tersely: 'Just remember what I've said and maybe you'll keep out of trouble.'

'I'll remember.' Rod gigged his mount, brushing the other aside. He felt a strange dislike of the man and the feeling that Ferris was in this dirty deal up to his neck was growing stronger in his mind every minute. It was a strange brand of law that seemed to be handed around in Twin Ranchos. It needed a strong and upright man to keep peace and order here; a man such as his brother had been, and with Hank's death, there was little here to keep order. Ferris was not a man to keep the lawless element under control, especially if there was someone bigger than he was, giving orders from above. Judging by the conversation he had overheard, that was the way of things.

Glancing over his shoulder, he noticed that the deputy was on the boardwalk on the other side of the street, still watching intently. Rod felt a little wave of anger pass through him. Then it was gone from his mind as he turned, faced along the street. The town seemed uneasy, he thought tightly, as he walked his mount along the main street. Whether it was always like this, or had been only since his brother had been killed was something he did not know. But it was something he could sense, something in the air, tension that crackled on the faint breeze. He reckoned it would take very little to start guns firing here.

He was almost at the far end of the street now. Here, there were only small tumble-down shacks on both sides, low-roofed buildings, many in an advanced state of decay. A deserted, abandoned part of town, he thought idly, letting his gaze roam over the buildings. When there had been a movement back to the town, following the discovery of gold in the hills, new buildings had been thrown up and others, built when the town had been erected here, had been left to rot and fall apart.

His horse whinnied softly, head coming up sharply. It was more of a warning of danger to him than any other sound or movement could have been. Swiftly, he looked about him, seeking out the reason for his horse's sudden alarm. He could see nothing moving in the multitude of dark shadows that lay among the buildings around him.

There was scarcely any sound to give away the position of another horse, a crouching figure; yet he knew, more surely than anything that someone was there, even though he could not see him.

The thought had scarcely passed through his mind when the sharp crack of a gunshot shattered the stillness. His horse reared instinctively at the sudden sound and the movement undoubtedly saved his life. The bullet passed within an inch of his chest, nicking the bridle in its flight. Savagely, he dug spurs into the horse's flanks, felt it respond at once, leaping forward, its feet scuffing up the dust of the street. Another shot rang out, but the gunman was firing too quickly now to take proper aim and the fact that he had missed his first shot seemed to have unnerved him sufficiently to spoil his aim.

Sliding from the saddle on the opposite side to where the gunman lay hidden, Rod ran forward, jumped for the boardwalk and threw himself flat on the mouldy wood, the smell of rottenness and decay in his nostrils, striking the back of his throat. Carefully, he lifted his head and peered about him, searching with eyes and ears for the bush-whacker. The other had stopped firing once Rod had gone down under cover, not wishing to give away his position.

Wriggling forward, Rod reached the end of the building. In front of him, the boardwalk stopped. Reaching out with his left hand, he picked up a stone and tossed it out into the mouth of the alley. It struck the bottom of one of the walls on the other end with a hollow sound, drawing another shot that kicked up dirt a few yards away. The sound of the explosion told Rod that the gunman was hiding somewhere along the alley, possibly only a few yards from the mouth, where it joined the main street. The moment he moved out of cover, he would be inviting a bullet in the head.

He lay there for several seconds, thinking things over in his mind, then glanced behind him, twisting his head around with a wrench of neck muscles. The door of the building lay half open, hanging on bent, rusty hinges. He moved to his feet, eased himself back noiselessly and slipped inside the building. For a moment, he paused there, trying to guess the other's actions. The would-be killer was probably holed up in one of the buildings and was not likely to shift his position. Therefore, Rod crept forward through the room which overlooked the street, setting one foot down in front of the other, testing the floor. The smell of the deserted place came to him more strongly now, a sharp-bitter smell in his nostrils. There was a door at the far side of the room, open, but with the floor there littered by rubbish. This must have been a store-room at some time in the past for through the doorway, he could just make out a jumble of cases piled carelessly one on top of the other. Letting his weight fall slow and easy, so as not to creak any of the boards underfoot, he passed through into the rear room. There was a dust-covered window at the back which he guessed overlooked the alley. It was towards this that he made his way, moving slowly and with extreme caution. It only needed one slight mistake on his part, for him to bring down more gunfire on himself.

Something brown and furry scurried across the floor, vanished through a hole gnawed in the wall. It was the only sound, the only movement he detected.

Reaching the far wall, he pressed himself tautly against it, glanced sideways through the window. The faint sunlight which managed to filter down into the narrow alley, was reflected off the layer of grey dust on the glass, making it difficult to see anything through the window. Then he heard the hidden gunman move, out in the alley. A moment later, he saw him, edging forward to the other side of the narrow opening. He had obviously moved out of one of the buildings there and his anxiety and curiosity had got the better of him; either that or the strain had proved too much for him and he was moving forward to try to locate Rod.

Grinning a little, Rod recognized the other as the weasel-faced man who had been talking with Ferris in the other's office. He had found him a lot sooner than he had anticipated. He paused for a moment, waited until the other had drawn level with the window, waited a moment longer, watching the other's crouched stance and the gun held in his right hand. Then he lifted his own weapon, smashed the tip of the barrel into the glass and called out sharply

'All right, mister, that's far enough. Now drop that gun and lift your hands.'

He saw the other jerk at his words, almost as if he had been struck physically. For a second, the thought of further action lived on the other's face, then he let the revolver fall from his hand and straightened up, lifting his hands slowly, reluctantly over his head.

'That's better.' Easing his legs over the window ledge, Rod dropped into the alley, moved over to the other, coming up behind him. Jabbing the barrel of the .45 into the man's back, he lifted the other gun from its holster and tossed it down into the dirt.

The man said hoarsely: 'You got this all wrong, mister.' His voice had a grating, whining edge to it.

'Whatever you were thinking of doing, don't try it,' Rod warned as the man lowered his arms. 'You're as close to your Maker as you'll ever be right now. I don't like bush-whackers shooting at me from ambush.'

The man swallowed thickly. There were tiny beads of sweat on his forehead, some rolling down into his eyes. His breathing was tense and ragged. The noise was loud in the quiet alley. 'You got the wrong man, stranger,' he said tensely. 'I heard shooting and came along to take a look. That's why I had my gun m my hand. I wasn't goin' to take any chances on meetin' up with anybody who might be out there on the street.'

'You're lyin',' Rod said thinly. 'And what's more, you're not doin' it very well. You tried to shoot me down and when you didn't hear any further sound you figured that maybe you'd been luckier than you deserved and you'd managed to drop me, but you had to be sure. So you came creepin' along the alley to see what damage you'd done.'

'No, that's not the way of it at all,' persisted the other. He shook his head rapidly.

'Maybe I should tell you that I overheard some of your conversation with Ferris the other night, just before I knocked on the door of his office. You two polecats are in some dirty deal right up to your necks. Wouldn't surprise me if you weren't in on the deal that ended with my brother bein' killed.'

'Your brother?' Rod felt the jasper's back muscles stiffen as he finally realized who was behind the gun.

'That's right. And don't tell me that you didn't know who I am. Seems to me there are too many people in town tryin' to kill me just as they did Hank. Only forewarned is forearmed and you won't find it quite so easy to get rid of me.'

'I don't know what you're talkin' about,' muttered the other sullenly.

'No? Let's take a walk back along the alley a little way. I figure there are some ways of makin' a critter like you talk.'

He saw the look of fear that flashed over the man's face and went on relentlessly. 'Now turn around and walk back to the end of the alley. Remember there are six tickets to hell in this gun and any one of them can put you six feet under at Boot Hill.'

The man turned, threw a quick glance up at Rod, then stepped past him and moved back along the alley. He held his hands stiffly by his sides now, glanced down at one of his guns lying on the ground, the metal glinting brightly in the dim sunlight. Rod noticed the direction of the other's glance, grinned tautly. 'Go ahead and pick it up, *hombre*,' he said grimly. 'I'll give you a better chance than my brother got.'

'You must think I'm a fool,' said the other harshly. 'I've heard a little of you, mister. They say you're faster than your brother was. It would be cold-blooded murder if I tried any trick like that.'

'Then keep right on moving. I figure you've got a lot of talking to do.'

'I've told you I don't know anythin'.'

Rod prodded the other hard in the back with the gun, thrusting him towards the far end of the alley. The man's thin shoulders slumped forward fractionally as he advanced along the alley, keeping well in to one side. Rod smiled grimly to himself, recognizing the motion. The other was beaten and knew it. There ought to be little difficulty getting information out of him.

Then, suddenly, the other's hand moved, grabbing sideways, not towards his belt, but towards a holster under his left armpit. He swung sharply, bringing up the small but deadly Derringer, squeezing the trigger in the same sweeping movement. Rod jerked himself to one side instinctively, cursing himself for his inattention in not searching the other more thoroughly when he had relieved him of the other Colt. The bullet lanced along the side of his head as he pulled to one side. It was as if a redhot poker had been laid along his scalp; stunning him. He half dropped to his knees, squeezed off one shot at the blurred figure in front of him, as the other began to run, his feet clattering on the stones in the alley. Spinning darkness threatened to swoop down on Rod as he knelt there, one hand outstretched against the wall beside him in an attempt to steady himself and prevent him from falling forward onto his face. He had the inescapable conviction that if he fell, the darkness would engulf him completely and whatever he did, he must not let that happen. He had to hang onto his buckling consciousness, get to his feet and go after the other. The man was his only lead and he must not let him out of his sight.

He made a futile attempt to sweep away the encroaching shadows that swirled around him, slumping down onto his hands and knees, head hanging between his arms. He shook it savagely, ignoring the pain which lanced through his skull, threatening to split it asunder. Somehow, he managed to fight off total unconsciousness, thought he heard voices penetrating the thunder in his ears. His head throbbed painfully and the blood hammered across his forehead, bringing tears into his eyes, half blinding him.

With a tremendous effort, he succeeded in pushing himself up to a sitting position. The houses around him were spinning dizzily and there was a rising feeling of nausea in the bottom of his stomach which was thrusting its way up into his chest in spite of everything he could do to keep it down.

Placing one hand on the wall, he stood up, swaying groggily, licking his lips, swallowing in an attempt to force down the sickness. The alley that stretched away in front of him was empty. There was no sign of the man who had tried to kill him. But even as he stood there, peering dazedly about him, he heard the sound of a horse starting up into a run less than a hundred yards away.

Drawing a breath of air down into his tortured lungs, gagging a little as it almost chocked him, he staggered back into the main street, caught up the bridle and hauled himself up into the saddle. He almost fell from the horse as weakness swept over him. Grimly, he hung on, tightening his lips, twisting his fingers into claws as he strove to maintain his grip on the reins. Slowly, his head was beginning to clear. He could feel the warm trickle of blood down his cheek from the wound of the near-miss and winced as he touched it gingerly with his fingertips.

That bullet had almost ended his life, and it had been nothing more than his own carelessness which had caused it. He should have made absolutely certain that the other had been disarmed before allowing him to lower his arms. Wheeling his mount, he rode into the alley, let his horse pick its own way around the debris that littered it at the far end. In the dust he made out the tracks of a horse, unmistakable where the dust had lain undisturbed for many years. Evidently this part of Twin Ranchos was even less frequented than he had imagined.

Shaking off the effects of the scalp wound, he followed the clear trail to the edge of town, saw that the rider had cut out over the country there, keeping away from the main trail. It meant that he was riding through rough country, but it also meant that it ought to be reasonably simple to follow his tracks here.

He set his mount at a quick lope. From the tracks, where the hooves had dug deeply into the soil, it was apparent that the man he was pursuing was riding fast, determined to get to where he was heading in the shortest possible time. It meant that he would not be taking too many precautions about checking to see whether or not he was being followed. The trail led him through brush, thorn and mesquite, then along a narrow, steep-sided ledge where it was difficult to follow it on the hard rock, and then down into a broad valley, covered with ankle-deep grass, the hoofprints of the bushwhacker's horse clearly visible in the soft earth.

Half an hour later, as he topped a low rise, he reined up sharply. The other was less than two miles distant, clearly visible against the sunlit background of the valley. He had clearly ridden hard to build up such a lead, but Rod did not hurry. He could visualise the moves which the other would make during the next few hours. The hills were in the distance, on the western skyline, lifting tall and rough against the heavens. It would take the man more than five hours of hard riding to reach the foothills and until he did, unless he swung sharply off this trail, he would follow a clearly-defined trail.

Moving upgrade, a little way off the trail, he rode into thin timber, first-growth pine that lifted tall and straight towards the cloudless blue of the sky. Here, he was out of the direct rays of the glaring sun and the trees seemed to keep out some of the heat too for there was a certain coolness in the air under the green umbrella of boughs and leaves that were interlaced overhead into a thick canopy.

At intervals, there was a gap in the trees, through which he could look down and follow the gunman's movements. So far, the other was behaving exactly as he had anticipated. Shortly before noon, he saw the man pause on the banks of a stream and get down from the saddle. Once or twice, the other looked behind him as he let his horse drink and before climbing back into the saddle, he moved on foot to the top of a rising knoll of ground, shaded his eyes and scrutinised the backtrail for any sign of pursuit.

Eventually, he seemed to be satisfied and mounted up once more, riding on to the west. Rod let him widen the distance between them a little before moving on himself. At the moment, he wasn't sure what the other was up to, where he was riding. But there was a method behind it all, Rod had no doubt on that score. He threw a quick, calculating glance at the sky. It would be dark before the other reached the hills, he reckoned. He would have to take the risk of riding up closer to him when dusk came, or he might lose him in the darkness. Out here in the open, it was possible to keep him in sight for several miles, but there were many trails in the hills and it would be too easy for the other to throw him off the scent, even unintentionally, not knowing he was being trailed.

The long afternoon passed slowly. The sun lifted to the zenith, then began its slow wheel westward. Dust blew up off the plain and Rod reversed his neckpiece over his mouth and nose, lowered his head, leaning forward in the saddle, easing the weight on the horse.

At six o'clock, the country lifted from its flatness. He spotted the gunman in the distance, with the sun ahead of him, just moving up towards the river that came down from the hills and flowed over the plain to the north. From where he sat, it looked as if the other was making a meal for himself, resting up his horse for a ride into the hills.

Circling around, Rod managed to get within a quarter of a mile of the other without being seen. The man was seated on a low rock, his back to him, teasing some meat with the tip of his knife, occasionally thrusting it into his mouth and chewing on it, washing it down with water from his canteen. Rod tightened his lips as he kept down under cover. It would have been so easy to take the other now and every nerve and fibre in him urged him to do so, but he resisted, forced the feeling away. At the moment, he was not concerned as much with killing this man as he was with following him to wherever he was headed. Unless he missed his guess, the gunman was riding out to report to someone and the belief that it might be the outlaw, Booth, was growing stronger in his mind every minute.

He settled down to wait patiently as the sun dipped behind the tall mountains and sent its final burst of orange and scarlet into the heavens, leaving the plain cool and blue with the coming of night.

The man seated by the river gave no sign that he knew he had been trailed all of that day and slowly, Rod felt some of the tightness in him beginning to ease a little. His shoulders were pulled up tense, and he forced himself to relax. The minutes ticked by slowly. The other seemed in no hurry to be on his way again. Then the man got heavily to his feet, moved over to where his horse stood beside the river and bent to tighten the cinch. This done, he brought water in his hat and tossed it onto the small fire he had built. There was a brief swirl of grey smoke.

Climbing into the saddle, the other rode through the river, up the opposite bank and then set off at a steady pace for the hills. Rod watched him go, waited patiently until he was almost out of sight in the deep shadow of the hills, then put his own horse over the river. The current caught at it strongly in the middle of the river, but the bay was a sure-footed brute and Rod felt no fear as it picked its way across the smooth, treacherous stones on the river-bed.

Halfway up, the slope leading onto one of the rocky ledges, the trail veered suddenly to the right. Rod paused, uncertain, for a moment, sensing a trap. It had been too easy trailing the other and he had the feeling that maybe the man was not as green as he had seemed, that he may have either spotted him early in the day or guessed he might follow him when he came round, and had deliberately made it easy for him to catch up on him so that he might lead him into another ambush and this time, the gunman would not make the same mistake that he had before.

The shale crunched and slid under his horse's feet as he urged it upgrade. He was making too much noise here, he told himself fiercely but it was quite unavoidable. He figured that if the man had continued riding and was not intent on setting up a deadfall for him, he was perhaps five hundred yards ahead, moving upgrade too through the foothills.

He could still make out the trail; at first, the marks of hooves were clear in the sand and thin soil, but further on, where they led over rocky ground, they were not so easy to follow. Soon, as the darkness increased, he was left with scarcely any trail to follow. Five minutes later, he entered the narrowness of a defile, moved through it slowly and carefully, keeping his gaze moving from side to side, alert for trouble. If there was to be any ambush, this was where it would have been set up for him, he thought with a growing conviction, but nothing happened and he rode out into the open once more, looked about him, then drew back into the shadows instinctively as the sound of voices reached him from somewhere just up ahead. Swiftly, he leaned forward in the saddle, placed his hand over his horse's mouth to prevent it from giving them away, and slid softly from the saddle.

At first, he could make out nothing in the darkness of the rocks. Slowly, he edged forward, probing the dimness with his glance, pushing his sight ahead of him as far as he was able.

A moment later, he realized that he was standing on the edge of a wide clearing, and that there was a tumbledown shack built against a smooth rock wall. He smelled smoke as he crouched there on one knee, knew that he had reached his destination. There was a brief glow of yellow light as the cabin door was opened, he caught a glimpse of two figures limned against the light, then there was darkness again.

FOUR
The Big Kill

An hour afterwards, the moon rose, lifting high into the eastern sky, round and full, a bright yellow colour which gave enough light to see by although not quite enough, as yet, to be sure of what one saw. Rod ran the tip of his tongue along his lips. During the hour he had been watching the place, there had been no further movement and he guessed the two men had settled down there for the night. Tethering his mount to one of the overhanging branches, he made his way cautiously forward. There were two horses on the far side of the cabin, but neither of them moved as he slipped closer to the ramshackle building. There was a single window in one wall but some lengths of tattered cloth had been drawn over it so that until he was close up to it, it was impossible to see any light through it.

Against the wall, he waited patiently, feeling cold and hatred come to him as he remembered how the ferret-faced man there had tried to gun him down in that alley in Twin Ranchos. Pressing his ear close to the wall, he was able to make out the vague murmur of voices, but for all its broken-down appearance, the cabin had deceptively

79

thick walls and it was impossible to make out any of the words. He could only ascertain that there were two men in there, talking quietly between themselves.

Moving around the wall on soft feet, he reached the door. For the first time, he noticed that it was slightly ajar, a thin strip of yellow lamp light showing against the edge. From his vantage point here, he was able to hear what was being said inside the cabin.

The ferret-faced man said harshly: 'I still think we ought to wait for a while before we try to finish him, Booth. He's a dangerous character and there ain't a man in the territory who'll go up against him in fair fight. Maybe not a man in the whole of the west.'

A rougher, snarling voice which he guessed belonged to Booth said thickly: 'Maybe not, but he's only one man like his brother was. We could lay a deadfall for him, stake out a couple of men in town.'

'That's what Ryan and that other *hombre* tried to do on the trail from Hatchet Bend and you heard what happened there?'

'Ryan is a fool,' said the other contemptuously. 'He left too much to chance. But if we can get Ferris to do as he's told, it might be even easier. It shouldn't be too difficult to get some charge brought against this critter. Once he's in jail, we can arrange to have a lynch mob ready to move in and bust him out. A rope over a tree and that will be the end of him.'

There was a pause, then the ferret-faced man said tightly: 'I've been takin' the time to talk things over with Ferris. He's scared now. Reckon Wellman's appearance in town has rattled him more than he wants to admit.'

'Then it might be time to get ourselves a new lawman in Twin Ranchos,' grunted Booth. 'I've had my doubts about Ferris for some time.'

'Won't be difficult,' said the other confidently. 'As soon as we get Wellman out of the way, we can do that. But this *hombre* is gettin' a mite dangerous to us. Snoopin' around and askin' questions.'

'Are you sure he didn't follow you out here?'

'Of course I'm sure. I tell you that if I didn't kill him, I creased his skull for him with that bullet. He'd have been out for hours.'

'Why didn't you stick around and make sure of the job?' demanded Booth. 'You had him there. You could have shot him down and that would have been the end of it.'

'Anybody could have heard those shots and come arunning to see what the trouble was. I didn't want to take that risk. Besides, I figured you'd want to know how things are in town.'

Rod decided that he had heard enough. Hefting the Colt into his right hand, he reached out with his left, placed his palm flat against the edge of the door, then thrust it in with a sharp shove. Quickly, he stepped inside, jerking up the gun to cover the two men seated at the long wooden table in the middle of the cabin. The man seated beside Ferret-face was broad, with craggy, granite-like features and pale blue eyes that narrowed instantly as Rod burst into the room. His right hand moved down towards his waist, then stopped, frozen in mid-air, as Rod's voice cut through the tense silence.

'I'd like you to go for it, Booth.' He stepped forward a couple of paces, taking in everything in the room with a single, all-encompassing glance. 'It will give me the greatest pleasure to cut you down right here and now. Save me the trouble of takin' you back into Twin Ranchos and having you strung up from a tree.'

Booth glared at him, dark colour diffusing his features. Then he drew back his lips into an animal-like snarl. 'You'd never get me arrested, even if you did manage to get me back to Twin Ranchos.' There was a note of confidence in his voice.

Rod smiled thinly. 'Because you figure that your friend, Deputy Ferris, wouldn't dare arrest you?' He shook his head slowly. 'I'd hang you myself, Booth and I doubt if anybody would lift a finger to stop me.'

The other tightened his lips at that, evidently recognized that Rod meant every word he said. He lifted his hands and placed them flat on the table in front of him. But there was still menace in every line of his body and Rod knew he would go for his gun the slightest chance he got.

'As for you, friend.' Rod swung to face the other man at the table. 'I rather guessed you were in this up to your neck. Now I know just how deep you are. You figuring on joinin' Booth here at a hanging party?'

'You couldn't do it,' said the other, but his tone had lost a lot of its confidence. 'There ain't a single man in town who would back you if you tried that.'

'Supposin' I was to take you into Hatchet Bend. Could be there's justice there.'

For the first time, he noticed a little took of apprehensive fear creep into the man's face. Booth seemed unconcerned with that possibility. 'Reckon you ought to know there's quite a reward out for Booth's capture, dead or alive. So far, I don't recollect seein' your picture around on any of the wanted posters.'

'Keep your mouth shut,' said Booth warningly to the other. 'Can't you see that he's only tryin' to rattle you into talkin'. He knows nothin' and that's the way it's goin' to stay.'

'This gun says that it isn't,' Rod said warningly. 'I came here lookin' for the snake who killed my brother. If I have to shoot down men like you to get at the truth, even if you had no hand in it, then I'll do it. Nobody is goin' to miss either of you.'

'I'll tell you what you want to know,' broke in the thin-faced man. There was a sheen of sweat on his forehead and his hands were gripping the edge of the table tightly, the knuckles standing out whitely with the pressure he was exerting. Before Booth could say anything more, could even move, he went on hurriedly: 'Like you say, there ain't any posters with my picture on 'em. And if there is a reward for Booth, then I figure I might as well claim a share to it and —'

He broke off sharply. Too late, Rod saw that his talk had been a feint, to take his attention off him, to make him believe that Booth was the dangerous one of the two. Without warning, he had heaved upward with both hands, hurling the table over against Rod. The nearer edge struck him on the knee, knocking him backward, off-balance. He went crashing against the wall at his back, striking it hard with his shoulders. Somehow, even though taken completely by surprise, he managed to keep a grip on both guns.

Both Booth and the other had risen to their feet as soon as the table had gone over. The lamp which had been resting on it had hit the floor, the glass shattering into a hundred pieces, the oil flowing out, bursting into flame as it ran across the floor, licking at the wall a couple of feet from where Rod lay.

Through the smoke and the flame which leapt up as the dry wood caught like tinder, he saw Booth go for his gun. Swiftly, instinctively, he triggered off a couple of shots at the outlaw, saw the man stagger as a slug took him in the shoulder. Then Booth had turned, running for the door, his body bent over in a low crouch to present a poor target.

The other man was still standing behind the overturned table. His face was alight with a feral glow, lips drawn back to reveal the uneven teeth. The red glow of the flames shone off his sweat-streaked features as he brought up his gun and lined the barrel on Rod's chest. Without pausing to think, without taking any notice of Booth, aware only that the other had reached the door and was jumping out into the night, he snapped up a quick shot at the man behind the table. Both guns seemed to roar at exactly the same instant of time. The noise was deafening inside the confined space of the room.

Rod felt the bullet pass his cheek, embedding itself in the wooden wall near his head. His own shot tore at the gunman's sleeve. Then, before he could fire again, the other had jumped the table, his feet slamming against

Rod's arm, hammering it hard against the floor. He was forced to release his hold on the gun as pain jarred up into his body. Sucking back on the shout of pain that rose to his lips, he fell back, kicking up with his feet as he went.

More by luck than judgment, his foot caught the other's arm, knocking the gun from his grasp, sending it spinning into the corner. Through blurred eyes, Rod saw the flames leaping higher now, between himself and the door, climbing towards the low ceiling. Once that caught, he would be trapped here. He strove to get to his feet, but the other hung onto him like a madman, throwing punches at his head and chest.

His right arm was still virtually useless where the other's boots had rammed into it, pinning it to the floor. He could feel the tremendous impact of the heat on the side of his face and the loud, roaring crackle blotted out almost everything. The gunman had his face pressed close to Rod's and he could feel his breath on his face. The man's weight was holding him down to the floor and with the table in front of him, there was very little room in which to manoeuvre. He tried to roll over onto his side, to throw the other off, but the other clung to him savagely. A tightly-bunched fist crashed into the side of his face, grazed the flesh on his cheek as he jerked his head on one side. Gasping, he managed to get his left arm free, thrust it up at the other's face, fingers reaching for the eyes. Either the other man died or he did. The killing fever showed in the gunman's eyes and he came boring in, anxious to finish this fight as quickly as possible. Jabbing, Rod caught the other on the nose, then gouged for the eyes. The man screamed as Rod's stiffened fingers found their mark. He hauled his head back, easing his hold.

Seizing his chance, Rod thrust up with all his strength, throwing the other off. The man fell over onto his side, rubbing at his eyes, face twisted into a grimace of agony. He lay there for a moment, sucking air down into his lungs, then came upright with a quickness surprising in a man who had taken as much punishment as he had.

Smashing rights and lefts to Rod's face, he aimed a heavy kick with his boot at the other's head, but Rod sensed it coming and jerked his head aside so that the blow landed on his shoulder. Even so, the pain that lanced through his arm was so intense that he almost cried out with the agony of it.

Fighting to retain a hold on his consciousness, aware now that the cabin was well alight, blazing like a torch in places, knowing that if he wanted to get out and not be roasted like an ox over a spit, he had to finish this man quickly, he forced himself to twist and kick out. His boot grazed along the other's thigh, threw him off balance so that he fell back against the side of the heavy table. Half-stunned, the gunman lay there, blinking his eyes, the muscles of his throat corded with the strain. By the time Rod got to his feet and managed to get a little feeling back into his badly bruised arm, the other had staggered upright, came rushing in with a series of wild swings, but Rod succeeded in stepping inside them, driving the other back until he was almost in the flames that formed a crackling barrier between them and the door.

For the first time, the other seemed to realize their danger. He half turned, saw the fire that blazed at his back and screamed once, thinly. Then he staggered drunkenly as Rod's fists beat a savage tattoo on his chest and face, toppled backward into the flames. Weak, sickened by the heat, Rod moved blindly forward, scarcely able to see, not really knowing if he was moving in the right direction. Bending he hooked his fingers around the other man's collar, dragging him forward with him across the burning floor. Blundering against the wall, he felt along it with his free hand, trying to find the doorway. His lungs were on fire with the heat, his face seemed blistered by the flames and the smoke got into his throat and eyes, making it impossible for him to see anything. In his ears, the roaring of the flames blended with the booming roar of the blood rushing through his veins and he felt his head swimming. Once he lost his hold on the man at his feet, was on the

point of going on without him, remembering that the
other had tried twice to kill him, had brought all of this on
his own head. Then he fumbled in the fire, found him and
managed to go forward another couple of feet. It seemed
that he could not possibly make it, not even if he did leave
the other to die here in the fire. Then, the smoke cleared
briefly and he was able to see the open doorway a little to
his left, staggered towards it, lungs bursting as they tried,
and failed, to get sufficient oxygen from the superheated
air for their needs.

Cool air swirled about him as he stumbled out into the
open. Dimly, he was aware of the clatter of hooves in the
near distance, but it was impossible to see anything, even
though a part of his mind told him that Booth had seized
his chance and was getting away while the going was good.
He stood for a long moment, drawing the pure, cold night
air down into his heaving lungs. Gradually, he was able to
breathe properly and see through the tears that obscured
his vision.

Glancing down, he saw that the gunman was still lying
at his feet, his clothing blackened and smouldering in
places where he had been dragged through the flames.
Bending, he turned the man over, stared down into the
smoke-blackened face, the wide-open, staring eyes, felt for
the pulse, but knew with a sudden certainty, even before
he grasped the other's wrist that there was no heartbeat.
The man who had tried his damnedest to kill him, was
dead.

With an effort, he got to his feet. The cabin was well
ablaze now, burning like a beacon in the clearing. He reckoned the fire would be visible for miles, although it was
unlikely there would be anyone else around to see it, apart
from Booth, somewhere in the moonlit darkness and
possibly one or two prospectors higher in the hills.

Slowly, he went over to where he had left his horse.
Swinging up into the saddle, he moved to the edge of the
clearing and stood looking down where the trail wound in
a series of switchback curves around the side of the hill,

plainly visible in the flooding moonlight that touched everything now with a cold, ghostly radiance. Off to one side, perhaps half a mile away, he was just able to make out the shape of the solitary rider, spurring his mount at a breakneck speed along the downgrade trail. Gritting his teeth, ignoring the pain and weakness in his body, gripping onto the reins with hands that felt burned and blistered, he put his own mount to the trail and rode out after Booth. How far the other would run, or where he would be able to run to, he did not know; nor did he care. All he knew was that he would follow the other as far as necessary, would shoot him down once he got him in his sights.

An hour before dawn, with the moon still hanging round and yellow in the sky and most of the stars still visible, powdering the heavens with a fainter light, Rod set his mount at a long meadow of wild grass that lay for perhaps a mile in front of him. He had seen nothing of Booth for the past half hour, although he knew the other was still ahead of him, still following this trail. Whether Booth knew that he was still alive and trailing him, he neither knew nor cared. In the moonlight it was not easy to pick out the other's sign, but here the rough grass had been broken and bent forward across the centre of the meadow where the other had ridden forward, pushing his mount to the limit. The trail which the other followed would, eventually, Rod realized, bring them back into Twin Ranchos, although by a very devious and circuitous route. He fell to wondering whether Booth was cutting back to the town on purpose, whether he figured that he could hide out there, that he would be safe from the law so long as Ferris was the deputy Sheriff.

At the far edge of the meadow, he splashed across a small stream that bubbled down from the hills at this point, picked up the trail on the far bank. There was no indication that Booth was attempting to cover his tracks. He had not ridden up or downstream to hide them and make them more difficult to follow. Either he was in too much of a hurry to do so, or he felt extremely confident that he was not being followed.

Rod smiled grimly to himself as he set his mount at a quick gallop. The other would soon discover how wrong he was, he told himself fiercely. He loosened his hold on the reins. His hands were beginning to sting where they had been burned, trying to drag the killer out of the fire. Blisters were forming on the palms and the backs.

Rolling himself a cigarette, he smoked it slowly. The pain in his throat had eased now and he was able to enjoy the smoke. Rocks jutted out of the slope in front of him. Rugged formations that seemed to have been carved by some idiot sculptor when the world began. There would be few trails leading through them, he decided, letting his glance wander over them, from one end to the other, and it would take a man several hours to find a way around them. The sign told him that Booth was riding straight on, had not deviated from the trail he had chosen some time back.

He touched rowels to the horse's flank, urging it on at a faster pace, wanting now to catch up with the other. Now that he could no longer see him, he began to get the feeling that maybe this was not Booth's trail he was following and he had somehow lost the killer in the dark.

Fifteen minutes later, swinging around a sharp bend in the trail, he found himself looking down into a narrow defile, saw the other directly ahead of him. He was riding more slowly now for in places the trail was only three or four feet in width and it needed only one mistake on the part of horse or rider, to hurl them into hell down two hundred feet of emptiness.

Reaching forward, he eased the Winchester from its boot, reined up the horse and sat tall in the saddle, sighting the weapon on Booth's back. The other was now well within killing range of the high-powered rifle, not more than a couple of hundred yards distant and he yelled loudly, the words carrying from one side of the rocky defile to the other.

'Hold it up there, Booth, or I'll kill you.'

It was a moment of decision for the outlaw and he made it without pausing to think. Reining up the horse, he turned it abruptly, wheeling it sharply to the right, to where an outjutting rock would afford him cover. Snapping the rifle hard into his shoulder, Rod loosed off two shots. The explosions were almost deafening as the echoes died away slowly. The horse below him moved in a wild lunge, somehow keeping its footing on the narrow trail. Then it had passed behind the rock and Rod drew in a sharp breath of disappointment. He had missed with both shots. He had had the other in his sights and yet he had somehow missed. His first shot had not missed entirely because of his own fault. Booth's horse had reared at the moment he had squeezed the trigger. But the second shot, a few moments later, ought to have hit him. There had been no excuse for missing then.

Now it was too late to kill him easily. The other had been warned and he would doubtless be ready for him, would make his stand somewhere along this narrow and treacherous trail.

He rode forward slowly, fed a couple more shells into the rifle, kept a tight hold of it as he neared the rock behind which Booth had disappeared. It was possible, he told himself grimly, that he had hit the other, but not where it would be sufficient to knock him down. Maybe Booth was lying wounded on the rocky floor of the trail. He looked across the fifty yards which separated him from the rock behind which he reckoned Booth to be lying in wait. The light in the east was brightening rapidly now and more and more details were becoming visible. Better relax, he told himself fiercely. His shoulders were humped tightly, but he soon found it was little use telling himself to relax, not with the knowledge that at any moment a rifle shot might put an end to him. Booth would not miss with his shot.

There was no sound now, except for the faint sighing of the breeze among the rocks and stunted trees.

Dismounting, he pressed himself close in to the rock, having put the rifle back into its sheath, pulling out one of the Colts. Very carefully, he peered around the corner of the rock. For a moment he found himself staring into the shadows there without really seeing anything. Then he realized that Booth was not there. Quickly, he scanned the rocks, knew that there was no place large enough for a horse to hide. Stepping along the trail, he glanced about him, then noticed the blood on the trail. It seemed to be almost continuous, following the trail, leading from where he had fired that shot downhill. He had hit Booth's horse. There could be little doubt about that and judging from the blood on the trail, the horse would not take Booth far. He turned abruptly, went back to his own mount, swung up into the saddle and went forward very slowly, his eyes and ears alert for the slightest movement and the faintest sound. He did not hurry, sure that Booth could not get far now. Here and there, patches of coarse brush grew up along the trail and he noticed how these had been crushed and flattened as the horse had lunged blindly through them. Judging by the sign, the horse was weaving erratically from side to side and it was clear that Booth was finding it difficult to control it.

A quarter of a mile along the trail, he came across Booth's horse. The other had ridden it right to the end. It lay near a small clump of bushes and one glance was enough to tell him that it was dead and he did not have to use a bullet to put it out of its misery. In a way, he felt glad of that. Not only would it have given away his position to Booth, but he disliked having to shoot a creature like this, even if only to put it out of its agony.

He cast about him for any sign of Booth. The outlaw was not far away now and in this sort of terrain it should be comparatively easy to pin him down, force him into a spot where it would be impossible for him to move.

He studied the terrain thoughtfully. From where he was now, he could look down on most of the surrounding countryside. The trail wound through the rocks, narrow and tortuous and he could cover almost every inch of it.

Dismounting, he moved to the edge of the trail. Below him, perhaps two hundred feet down, the sheer wall levelled out into a tumbled mass of rocks and boulders. There was no way of getting down there safely. Still, even if Booth was on the trail someplace, he could still move around to a limited extent and it would be risky pinning him down. His eyes caught the momentary movement among the rocks a hundred yards away, the figure darting from the rocks, running crounched low. The split second after he saw it, Rod fired. The bullet hit a boulder in front of the running figure, sent a flash of powdered rock from the top of it and Booth stopped running and dived for cover. Now it was a question of keeping him there, pinning him down so that he could not move without drawing a bullet.

He crawled along behind the cover of the rocks, then lifted his head slowly and peered down at Booth's position. There was no sign of the outlaw even from there. A little circle around, a move closer and he should be able to finish this satisfactorily, he thought grimly. By the time the sun was up, bringing the full daylight, this should all be over.

He found cover a couple of yards further on, peered down along the trail, saw the head that moved near the boulders, brought up the Winchester and loosed off three shots, scattering them around the boulder behind which Booth lay hidden. The head disappeared as the other dropped back into the narrow pocket among the rocks. His plan had worked. He had the other nailed now, unable to move to one side or the other, without exposing himself. Without a horse, Booth must surely know that he was finished, that it was only a matter of time before Rod got close enough to end it all.

Now we shall see just how good he is at waiting it out, Rod reflected. This was the time when one found out how good a man's nerves were, whether he had the patience to lie absolutely still, maybe for hours on end, waiting for the other man to make the first wrong move. Rod did not underestimate the other. Booth was, without doubt, a cunning and dangerous man. If he saw any way at all of turning the tables on him, he would do so.

Lifting the barrel of the Winchester, he laid it down flat on the rock in front of him, elbows raising him just enough to be able to see over the rocks in front of his position. The minutes dragged. Still no sign from Booth that the strain was beginning to tell on him. Easing himself over onto his side, Rod was content to lie there and let the deep, clinging silence of the hills go to work on Booth for him, eating like acid at his nerves until he felt like screaming, like scrambling to his feet and running forward, anything to end the silence and the uncertainty.

The dawn brightened, the grey light crept along the valley from the east as if a dark blanket were being rolled up. In front of him, the rocks formed a narrow cleft through which he was able to peer out and watch the spot where Booth had gone to earth, without any fear of the other being able to see him. Not unless he opened fire. And at the moment, he had no intention of firing first. He meant to let the silence and the waiting crack the other's spirit, eat at him until his nerves were shot to pieces. Then it would be the other who would open up first. Both parts of the trail on either side of the boulders below him were clearly visible to him and Booth was cut off from water and cut off from any possibility of escape. Without a horse, he was finished and he would know it.

By the time the sun rose, flooding the valley with a red glow, Rod knew that it was going to be another day of unbearable heat and from where he was lying, it looked as if Booth was in the worse position as far as the shade was concerned.

Rod waited and the time passed slowly. Booth would be trying to think of a way out of his predicament right now, he thought tensely; maybe wondering if there was a chance of making a break from where he now lay to a more favourable position from where he could perhaps circle around Rod and take him by surprise. Without a mount, that was his only chance of getting away from here alive. And the only horse in the vicinity was Rod's own bay.

An hour passed, then two. Still no sign from Booth that he was still alive. Then he started to do something. Without revealing himself, he yelled loudly:

'You still there, Wellman?'

For a moment, Rod felt startled at the other knowing his name. Then he realised that Ferret-face must have warned him who he was. Gently, he eased the rifle a little closer to him, tightening his grip on it, but did not answer. He wanted the other man to worry a little more before he died.

'I know that you're still hiding up there someplace, Wellman! Why the hell don't you answer me? Or maybe you're scared. Sure, that's it. You're plain yeller and they tried to tell me you were a fast man with a gun.'

Rod grinned tightly to himself as he lay hard against the rock, flat on his stomach, eyes slitted against the sunglare, watching the spot where the other lay. It was Booth who was getting scared now; there was no doubt about that, yelling in order to hear his own voice more than anything else.

A minute passed as silence settled itself once more over the trail. Rod eased himself noiselessly into the cleft of the rock, making his body a little more comfortable. He could hear Booth shifting himself below, although he could see nothing of him. Then the sunlight winked briefly on metal – the barrel of a rifle among the rocks and he nodded to himself. So the other was hoping that he might show himself, was he?

'You listen to me good, Wellman. I don't know why you're hunting me like this. But maybe if we was to take the time to talk this thing over quietly, we might see that we've both made a mistake about the other.'

The echoes of the other's words were thrown back into the valley from the rocky walls on either side. When he shouted again, there was a kind of desperation in the outlaw's voice.

'Just what do you hope to get out of killin' me,
Wellman? The reward money for my capture. There ain't
much to that.'

There'll be enough, thought Rod, to make up for some
of the things you've done in the past.

'Listen, I'll make a deal with you. I've got plenty of gold
stashed away in these hills, in places where you'd never
find it. Half of it's yours if you let me go. Enough to make
you rich for the rest of your life. My men were killed when
your brother brought that posse after us near the Little
Nugget mine. I didn't hold that against him. Reckon he
was only doin' his duty.'

So in spite of that, you decided to ride back into town
and shoot him down like a dog, without a chance to
defend himself, thought Rod with a growing tightness in
his mind. His fingers, curled around the rifle, seemed to
be congealed on the metal. Even now, he could feel the
tension inside him.

'You goin' to make that deal? I'll toss out my gun if you
say so.'

Still Rod remained silent. The other was getting edgy
now, his voice ragged and rising in pitch. Very soon, he
would start believing that Rod had ridden away, maybe
believing that Booth had died or been wounded. Wishful
thinking on his part, no doubt, but when a man plumbed
the bottom-most abyss of fear, he would believe anything.

High noon and still Booth lay out there, crouched
down behind the boulders. Rod felt a trickle of sweat form
on his forehead, run down onto the bridge of his nose,
itching and irritating as it ran down his cheek. He brushed
it away angrily with the back of his hand. The heat was
beginning to make itself felt now, burning all of the colour
out of the countryside, coming up at him in dizzying, sickening waves that blazed into his eyes, penetrating even
through tightly closed lids. Time and again, his eyes lidded
and closed and he almost drowsed off, only the sudden
jerk of the heavy rifle on his wrists bringing him back to
full alertness.

He was afraid that Booth might manage to slip away during one of these periods when he drowsed off.

Booth called: 'If you can still hear me, Wellman, I'm tellin' you to stand up and face me like a man and not try to shoot me down from under cover like a yeller-livered coward. I always had you figured for a topnotch gunfighter but it seems I was wrong. You're as yeller as your brother was.'

Rod felt the blood surge angrily along his veins at that last remark. For a split second, he was on the point of rising to his feet, moving in to kill the other for having made such a remark. Then sanity prevailed and he realized that Booth had merely said that to force him out into the open, knowing that an angry man was a rash one and more likely to make a mistake.

Grinning a little, lips drawn back, he called harshly: 'You're as good as dead right now, Booth. You can't get away without me seeing you and you've got no water. In your hurry to get away, you left your canteen with your mount, back there on the trail.'

He heard a faint curse from the hidden man. Then there was the sound of a boot scraping on rock as Booth shifted his position. The other was getting uneasy now, every nerve and fibre straining for action, for something to relieve the terrible silence and uncertainty.

Two shots rang out, close on the heels of each other. The bullets struck wide of Rod's position. Booth was rattled and firing blind, not knowing exactly where the other was. Carefully, Rod moved to one side. He was just able to make out the humped shadow of the other, lying flat on his stomach behind the boulders. He eased forward half a dozen yards and then stopped, eyes sweeping the area from side to side. He could picture Booth, lying there, squinting up against the savage glare of the sunlight, trying to see him before he opened fire on him, half-blinded by the sun, throat and mouth parched with thirst. Pressing close to the very edge of the trail where it would be difficult for Booth to see him, he left his rifle on the smooth ground and pulled one of the Colts from its holster.

If Booth had only the one gun, then he had only a couple of bullets left in it, he thought dryly, then pulled himself up short. That wasn't necessarily the case, he reminded himself. The other had had plenty of time in which to reload and counting bullets could be fatal.

Moving around the smooth curve of the rock, he reached a point where he was able to look down clearly at the other, saw the man's legs splayed out behind him as he hugged the ground, occasionally lifting his head to search the rocks of the trail. Grinning savagely, Rod lined up the Colt on the other's prone body, finger bar tight on the trigger.

'Booth!' he called loudly, sharply. 'Drop that gun and come on out.'

Savagely, the other jerked around to face him, eyes narrowed in his head as he tried to make out where he was. He was rolling in the same instant that he realized Rod had moved around to flank him. The gun in his hand spat flame and the slug tore the top from one of the boulders a foot from Rod's head. Taking careful aim, he squeezed the trigger, felt the gun jerk in his hand. In the harsh sunlight, he saw Booth trying to get to his feet as the slug hit him. For a moment he succeeded, striving to bring up the gun in his hand. Almost, he made it, the sunlight glinting on the barrel. Then he seemed to sag at the knees as if all of the life had gone out of him, and the Colt slipped from his nerveless fingers to clatter onto the rocks as he fell on top of it.

Knowing how cunning the other was, Rod advanced carefully on him, but Booth did not move as he walked into the small hollow where the other lay, face-downward in the grey dust. He touched the other's side with the toe of his boot, turning him over. Booth flopped limply onto his side. His face was grey, as if all of the blood had been drained from it, but he was still breathing, the air sighing in and out of his lungs with an odd rasping sound that was horrible to hear.

Booth's lips were drawn back, exposing his teeth in a snarling grimace and his eyes were fixed on Rod's face as the other bent over him. There was an expression in them which the other did not understand, almost as if the outlaw were secretly amused at something which he found funny.

'Might have been better if you'd given yourself up,' Rod said tightly.

With an effort, the other shook his head, grimacing at the movement. 'Only a rope waitin' for me, Wellman,' he said croakingly. 'Do you reckon I didn't know that? But they'll never hang Matt Booth.'

Rod gave a brief nod. There was no point in hiding the fact from the other. Booth knew well enough that he was a dying man, that it was only a matter of time. He seemed, however, to have something on his mind, for he tried to lift himself up onto his elbows, relaxing only when Rod gently, but firmly, pushed him back down with the flat of his hand.

'I know, I know,' grated Booth thinly. 'That slug was a little too close for me to have any chance even if you got me to a sawbones.' His brows drew together and his body jerked convulsively as a fresh spasm of pain lanced through him. 'Why did you come riding after me, Wellman? Was it something to do with your brother? Maybe you figured you had to finish what he left off.'

'I didn't know where I was being led when that *hombre* headed out of town leavin' a trail behind him that a blind man could follow in the dark,' Rod told him. 'But when you tried to kill me in the cabin, then I had to do this.' He paused, then went on harshly: 'Besides, there are a heap of people back in town who reckon you killed Hank. That after you escaped from that posse in the hills, you came back into town after dark, went along to the window of the hotel and fired through it at Hank as he lay on the bed.'

Booth stared fixedly at him for a long moment. His eyes were beginning to glaze over now and his throat muscles corded as he tried to speak. Quite suddenly, it seemed desperately vital that he should say something.

'You're wrong, Wellman. I didn't kill your brother. I never went back to Twin Ranchos after what happened in the hills. I wasn't goin' to risk gettin' myself shot after I'd lost all of my men. That would have been stupid.'

Rod remained bent over him, his head lifted a little, staring off into the sun-hazed distance. In spite of everything, he knew that Booth was telling him the truth. There was no need for the other to lie now, with death so close to him. He felt a deep and empty weariness in him, his brain hollow and strange. He seemed as far as ever from finding out who had killed Hank. The killer had to be somewhere.

'You ever killed a man before, Wellman?' The other jerked the words out through his lips.

For a moment, Rod lowered his gaze, staring down at the dying man, then gave a quick nod. 'I've killed a lot of men,' he said flatly, 'but I always gave them their chance. I never shot a man through the window of his room, without letting him go for his gun first.'

Swallowing thickly, the other whispered hoarsely: 'You'll have to kill a lot more men before you get to the end of the trail you've started ridin'. Mark my words, this is only just started, it's nowhere near finished.'

'I'll make sure that the man who murdered my brother dies before I do,' he declared harshly.

'Sure,' said the other in a sibilant whisper. 'And will you feel any better for it then? I've been a killer and outlaw most of my life. Believe me, it ain't worth it. There's always somebody on your tail waitin' to shoot you down. If it ain't the law, it's some bounty hunter out for the reward.'

'I reckon you've no need to worry about that now.'

A long sigh came from the other. He fell back onto the hard, rocky ground and his eyes turned up so that only the whites showed. For a moment, Rod thought he had died, but there was still a pulse beating weakly in his wrist. Then his head lolled to one side, his body seemed to loosen and relax. Matt Booth, outlaw and killer, was dead.

Slowly, Rod got to his feet, stood looking down at the other for a long moment. There was a deep and utter silence lying over everything and it was so still that he could hear the faint sound of his own mount cropping the tough, springy grass back on the trail a couple of hundred yards distant.

He buried Booth in the pock of ground close to where he had died, piled some of the smooth stones high over the shallow grave to keep off the coyotes and then went back to his horse, climbed up into the saddle, and took the trail which led back in the direction of Twin Ranchos. As he rode, he tried to turn events over in his mind, seeking some thread, no matter how slender, which would connect any of them and give him a clue as to the identity of the man who had shot his brother. But there seemed to be nothing to go on now that Booth was dead. The only other man he could think of was Jeff Carswell and yet even in his case, there were difficulties. He could not imagine the rancher having any cause to want Hank dead, even though Hank might have found out something about the rustling in the old days. Yet it was something he would have to check and he figured he knew a way of doing it.

FIVE
The Big Frame

From the top of the hill, looking down the grassy slope that lay spread out in front of him, Rod could see the ranch-house of the Triple Star ranch where it nestled in the hollow formed by the wide valley, bounded on three sides by the smoothly-sloping hills. It was an ideal place for a ranch, he thought, letting his gaze wander over the scene, drinking everything in. The hills would keep in the warmth during the spring and fall, and would keep out the cold winds of winter which came sweeping over the territory. In addition to that, the hills formed a natural protection for them, making it difficult for the ranch to be attacked by surprise.

Where the tall timber petered out, he came over the crown of the hill and put his mount to the slope, letting it move slowly, at its own pace. They had ridden hard for two days and a night and the horse was tired, but it still moved on without any complaint beyond a shake or two of its head. There was a corral and two barns near the house and the courtyard looked out over the nearby meadow where a small herd of cattle grazed peacefully. It was hard to realize that there could have been any trouble here. It was like a green oasis, set in the middle of a desert, he thought warmly, with trouble passing over it, not touching it at all.

Yet, if the girl had been right in what she had told him, Carswell had tried to take this ranch, had tried to rustle cattle and when that had failed he had deliberately run his own beef on the spread. He could see why other men might cast covetous eyes on the place and why the girl had been so anxious that he should make certain that Carswell ceased to bother them.

Riding into the courtyard, his mount kicking up little spurts of dust under its feet, he reined up in front of the porch. Almost at once, the door opened and the girl came out onto the porch, stood with one arm raised against a wooden upright, looking across at him. There was a half smile on her face, as if she were convinced that he had ridden out there only because he had changed his mind and would do exactly as she asked of him. A little of the tightness in his mind began to fade as he stepped down from the saddle and walked towards her, spurs dragging in the dust.

'I was half expecting you,' she said as he came up to her, stood with one foot on the porch. Her eyes took in the dust stains on his jacket and the dirt on his face from the smoke. He ought to have cleaned himself up at one of the streams he had crossed on the way there during the afternoon, he thought inwardly. 'Why did you come here? Have you thought over what I asked you in town?'

He gave a slow nod of his head. 'A little,' he said quietly, 'but a lot has been happenin' since then.'

'You'd better put your horse into the corral and then come inside and tell me about it,' she told him.

He moved back to the bay, turned it loose in the corral, closed the wooden gate and then walked back into the house. The girl was waiting for him in the small parlour, standing near the window, her hands clasped behind her back. She wore a brown skirt, belted at the waist with a broad, multi-coloured belt. Her white shirt was open at the neck, revealing the lovely lines of her throat as she faced him.

'I didn't notice many men out there when I rode in,' he

said quietly, nodding towards the open window. 'It might have been Carswell and some of his riders coming here instead of me.'

She smiled. 'You were let in,' she said confidently. 'You were seen as soon as you crossed the boundary fence. My men had orders to let you come here if they should ever see you on the trail.'

'You seemed very sure that I would come.'

Her smile widened a little and a brightness came to her eyes. Rod had the feeling that Julie Saunders could have a way about her which would make it difficult for a man to refuse her anything she asked for. 'You're still not sure about Carswell – about him being the man who either killed your brother or gave the order for him to be killed, are you?'

'A little while ago, if you'd asked me that question I would have said that I was very sure he wasn't the man.'

The girl sobered at that, took a step towards him, her face troubled. 'Something has happened since we met.' She laid a hand on his arm. There was nothing of coquetry about the movement, it had been merely a friendly gesture of genuine concern. 'What was it?'

'Somebody else tried to shoot me down in Twin Ranchos,' he said grimly. 'I trailed him out into the hills and he led me right to Booth.'

'Matt Booth – the outlaw your brother was hunting!' There was an expression of incredulity on her face and she puckered her brows in sudden thought. 'So he is still near town. We all felt so sure he would ride on, and never come back. Even the Mayor was certain of that. He apparently tried to tell your brother that there was nothing to be afraid of as far as Booth was concerned, any more.'

'Perhaps he was right about that.' The grimness in Rod's tone made her look at him a little more closely.

'Why do you say that?'

Rod touched his face gingerly as the memory of that fire which had destroyed the cabin surged up strongly in his mind. 'There was a gunfight in the hills. Booth got away but I managed to track him down. He's dead now, but before he died, he told me that he had not killed Hank, that he never returned into town after the outlaw gang was broken up.'

'And you think he was telling you the truth?'

'Yes, somehow, I'm sure he was. He knew he was dying, that he only had a few minutes left to live. There was no reason for him to lie.'

Nodding her head, she murmured: 'Then it must have been Carswell. There is no one else.' She sat down at the table, resting her arms on it, staring straight ahead of her. 'But you will still want proof before you do anything.'

'Yes,' he agreed flatly, without emotion. 'But I think I know how I might get that proof. If there is any tie-up with Carswell, I reckon I know where it might be.'

She gave him a keen glance, arrested by that remark. 'How do you intend to do that? Ride into Carswell's place?'

'Somehow I doubt if that would be wise. No, I think I'll pay a visit to the Sheriff's office in town. But I'll go there after Ferris has left, sometime during the night.'

'What do you expect to find there?' she asked in a tight, little voice.

'I'm not sure. Maybe nothing. But Ferris is in some dirty deal right up to his neck. The man who tried to kill me and Booth were talking it over in the cabin when I ran them to earth. Seems to me there's somebody higher up who is directin' things and if it is Carswell, there might be some evidence inside the safe in Ferris's office. Even if he hasn't kept it, my brother probably did. Could be that Ferris hasn't had time to go through all the papers yet and destroy anything that might incriminate him. If I can get my hands on them first, it could give me the information I want.'

She looked at him. 'When are you riding back into town?'

'Tonight. There's no time to waste. If word gets around about Booth's death, there could be all hell breakin' loose in town.'

'I'll get you something to eat before you go,' she said, getting to her feet and moving towards the door. 'And you'll be needing a fresh horse. You seem to have ridden some distance on that one out there.'

'I'd be mighty grateful,' he acknowledged.

She flashed him a quick smile, went through into the kitchen. While she was getting the meal ready, he went over to the window and stood looking out over the court-yard, the tall hills that lifted proudly on either side, with the trail along which he had ridden, just visible in the slowly-fading light. Night seemed to come reluctantly to this place, he thought musingly, almost as if it did not wish to hide any of the details of the scenery. It was a good place to live, a place where a man who had ridden too many trails might find peace and happiness. Almost savagely, he put the thoughts from his mind. He could not afford to dwell on things like that, he told himself fiercely. There was work to be done, and whether he liked it or not, it would have to be carried out to the bitter end, whatever that might be.

Twenty minutes later, Rod was seated at the long table in the dining room, facing a meal the likes of which he had not seen for many days. Only then did he realize just how hungry he really was, that he had not eaten for more than a day. He attacked the food with relish, washing it down with the hot coffee. Not until the plate had been filled for a second time, and then pushed away from him, clean, did he sit back in his chair, eyeing the girl across the table. 'Sure was a sample of fine cookin',' he said, 'and I'm mighty grateful. Now if you could let me have a fresh mount, I'll be ridin' on into town.'

'Do you have to ride out right now?' she asked in a little voice. 'It isn't dark yet and there may be someone watching the trail into Twin Ranchos.'

'It's a fair ride into town,' he reminded her. 'Don't worry none on my account. I'll keep my eyes open.'

'I hope so. Since my father died, I've had to do all of

the running of this ranch myself. Sometimes, it isn't easy
to get men to stay here and help me. Carswell has plenty
of influence and he can make it hard for a man to stick
around here.'

'I understand,' he said, nodding. Going out into the
courtyard, he waited while one of the hands brought a
horse from the stables, placed his own saddle on it and
tightened the cinch. Then he stepped up into the saddle,
gave the girl a brief nod, a smile, and ran on, out of the
courtyard and up into the stretching greenness of the
meadow. She stood in the porch and watched his figure
until he was on the far side of the meadow and climbing
the trail into the hills. For a moment she felt cold and
lonely. She had thought that she might be able to make
him do exactly as she wanted, without asking why. But this
man had a mind of his own, couldn't be easily swayed from
his own course of action. She hoped that he would take
care of himself and that he found what he was looking for
in the Sheriff's office. She told herself that she ought to
have warned him that Ferris could be cunning and treacherous in spite of his simple looks. But perhaps he already
knew that, she consoled herself. After all, if he had
managed to hunt down and kill Matt Booth, he must be
something of a gunhand himself.

She was not sure whether or not she liked that about
him. Turning, she went back into the house, shivering a
little although the evening air was far from cold. Closing
the door, she went up to her own room and stood in front
of the window, looking down over the courtyard and the
corral. Lifting her glance, she looked up towards the hills,
still touched by sunlight although the valley itself and the
ranch lay in shadow, but she could see no sign of Wellman
and after a moment she turned away, struggling with her
complex thoughts. For a moment she was not sure what
she wanted. Certainly this man had already killed, and if
he did find the man who had so brutally murdered his
brother, she would not blame him for killing again. She
tried to analyse her hatred of Jeff Carswell. Did it all stem

from the fact that he had tried to take over the ranch; or did it go deeper than that? At the time, it was something she could not have answered. She had permitted Wellman to see the depth of her hatred of the other and for a moment she experienced a faint thrill of apprehension. Then she put the thought away from her and lit the lamp on the table.

Twilight came on among the hills, lingered for a while, and then gave way to dark. Reaching the edge of the hills, Rod rode south, running on between twin rows of trees which soon became bunched more closely together until he was in deep, thick timber. Here he was protected from the main trail and although now and then he was forced to pull his mount to a walk as the undergrowth made it impossible to ride quickly, he made good time, hating the delay which these temporary periods caused. The feeling that he must soon come upon something which would tell him the identity of his brother's killer dominated him to the exclusion of everything else and for the time being there was really nothing else left in him but this desire for revenge. It had changed his life, had changed him in mind and spirit and body. No longer was he able to wake in the morning and feel clean and eager, as he had before that telegram had reached him. He could understand Julie Saunders wanting Carswell dead, but that made little impression on him, even though he knew she was looking to him to kill the rancher, was probably praying that Carswell was the man who had given the order for Hank to be killed, so that he would then have to kill him. He fell to wondering what this man Jeff Carswell was really like. Ruthless when it came to getting what he wanted, and when he had set his sights on something he allowed nothing or anyone to stand in his way. But that did not implicate him in Hank's murder.

Reaching a flat stretch of ground that lay for more than two miles in front of him, he touched spurs to his horse's flanks, felt it respond, running forward through the dusty grass. The cool night wind from the mountains blew down against him as he sat forward in the saddle. It soothed the pain in his face and he found himself eyeing the terrain around him with a renewal of interest, making out the major details in the faint light of the rising moon. He was high up now, and the air around him was cold and clear, with the stars beginning to stand out in the dark heavens like a powdering of silver dust, fading only where the lighter yellow glow of the rising moon showed on the eastern horizon. It seemed that he had climbed above most of the hills by taking this trail and now most of them seemed to be below him so that he was looking down on them with the valley running between them, clear to Twin Ranchos.

He passed a small cluster of old shacks laid out on either side of the trail as he reached the highest point and then began downgrade. They seemed empty and long deserted, split by the trail which went straight through them and a couple of hundred yards beyond them, set in the side of the hill, he saw the gaping black mouths of the mine workings. Nobody worked here now, he thought, reining up his mount for a moment and sitting tall in the saddle, listening to the silence which crowded in around him, pressing down on him from all sides.

Going downgrade, knowing he was within an hour's ride of Twin Ranchos now, he drifted forward with caution. Once, he thought he heard the steady drumming of a bunch of riders in the distance, but although he searched for them on all sides, he could make out nothing of them.

By the time he came within sight of Twin Ranchos, the moon was high, throwing a silver glow over everything, picking out the houses and buildings on either side of the street. He rode up onto a low bench of ground and sat his body carefully in the saddle, built himself a smoke, lit it, and watched the street below him, like a river of silver in the moonlight. Directly below him, there was one of the narrow alleys which led towards the main street, joining it less than ten yards from where he knew the Sheriff's office to be.

He could see no light in the Sheriff's office but the angle from which he was forced to view it making it difficult to be sure, he remained where he was for almost half an hour, watching and waiting. In all of that time, no one entered or left the office. Finally, he was satisfied. Lifting the reins once more, he gigged the horse forward, moved down into the dark alley. Tethering his horse at the end, he made his way forward on foot, picking his way carefully over the piles of rubbish and debris which littered the place.

Continuing on until he reached the corner of the building he crept along the side of its wall until he reached the boardwalk at the point where it intersected the alley and the main street. There was a pile of boxes and rubbish in the mouth of the alley and he almost blundered into them as he edged up onto the boardwalk, the wooden slats creaking ominously under his weight in spite of his effort to make no sound. He glanced along the street and saw nothing. A few lights showed in one or two of the buildings, but except for the hotel and the saloons, there were not many of them. Twin Ranchos, giving its trade to fugitives, those on the run from the law, made sure that its less desirable citizens had a more than even break.

He stood on the boardwalk in front of the Sheriff's office, body pressed tightly against the wall, acutely aware that he was exposed if anyone came out onto the street and happened to look closely along it. Standing quite still, he debated within himself whether to try to get in the front way, or move around to the rear in the hope of finding a door or window through which he might enter.

Now that he was in Twin Ranchos, he felt the deep-seated desire not to wait long. He had travelled too far, had hunted too long, only to meet up with the wrong men. Turning, he moved back into the alley, moved swiftly to the rear of the building. There were several small, square windows in this wall, he noticed, barred with strong bars of metal. This part of the building would be the jailhouse, he guessed. He began to doubt if he would find any mode of entry at this side. Stopping for a moment to listen, he cut in behind the building. There was a single door at the back which was locked – and, he guessed, bolted on the inside. No sense in trying to get in there. Methodically, he made his way along the wall, found the low window, its bottom edge less than six inches from the ground, partially obscured by rubbish.

Bending, he cleared the rubble away, making as little noise as possible, then gently began to push on the window. It gave slightly and he increased the pressure, almost falling off balance as it gave under his hands, pitching him forward.

It revealed a dark opening, beyond which he could see nothing. Squeezing his way through, he dropped a couple of feet onto a hard, earthen floor. There was a dry, musty smell in the air, catching at the back of his nostrils, with the odours of a thousand long-forgotten things blended with the smell of decay and rottenness. No sound came from the rest of the building and he reckoned he was safe enough to go on.

A faint light filtered in through the open window, just enough for him to be able to see by. There was a narrow partition on the far side of the small room, and easing his way towards it, he drew it carefully to one side. It rattled loudly in the silence of the room and he sucked air down sharply into his lungs as another two paces forward into the darkness, brought his outstretched hand into contact with a door. Sightlessly now, there being no light to guide him, he explored the wall here, felt the boards which seemed to have sprung loose from the wall, guessed that this was a storeroom for the office which was little used, with most of the junk piled inside and left to rot.

Opening the door which creaked on rusted hinges, he looked left and right, was able to see nothing, made a guess and went left, away from the rear of the building. The floor under his feet was no longer hard packed earth, but wood and once, a board moved under his weight and the creak, small though it was, seemed to ring throughout the whole length and breadth of the building. He stopped dead in his tracks, listening with a thumping heart for any movement but there was nothing, although a coldness ruffled the small hairs on the nape of his neck.

Sucking in a heavy gust of wind, he moved along the corridor that stretched away in front of him, and on either side, his outstretched fingertips touched at the metal bars of cells. He was inside the jailhouse and if this place had been built along the same lines as most of the others there should be a door at the end of this passage that led on into the outer office. Once inside, he would have to find where the confidential papers were kept. Maybe in a locked drawer of the desk, or in a wall safe. He hoped they were in a locked drawer. It would be easier to force that open, than it would a wall safe with probably a combination lock. Working on that would take him hours and he might still get nowhere.

He found the door he had expected to be there a few moments later. It was half open, there being no need for Ferris to lock this particular one. He paused for a few seconds, assessing the situation. It was unlikely that Ferris would return to the office that night, unless there was any trouble in town and he had to bring in a prisoner to lock up inside the jail. From his vantage point overlooking the place, everything had seemed reasonably orderly and quiet, although a gunfight could flare up at any moment. But that was a risk he would have to take.

Slipping through into the office, he made certain that the shutters were up over the windows and that there were no cracks near the door which would allow light to shine through into the street where there was a chance of it being seen by some late night reveller. His hand knocked against the lamp on the desk as he walked forward and he had to reach out and grab it quickly before it crashed to the floor. Gently, he set it back on the desk, stood between it and the door as he lit it. Deliberately he had turned the wick down as low as possible and only a faint yellow light came from it, scarcely touching the corners of the room, leaving them in shadow. He tackled the desk first. There were four drawers in it. The first one was open and inside he found several papers which were of no interest to him and a handful of posters bearing the pictures and rewards of several wanted men. Ferris seemed to have thrust them into the drawer as soon as he had received them, evidently not intending to take any action on any of them, even if the men came riding into Twin Ranchos. Many of these wanted men did ride here, he knew, knowing they had found a safe place in which to hide, so long as they did what Ferris or Carswell told them.

The remaining three drawers were all locked, resisted his efforts to pull them out. Taking the long-bladed knife from his pocket, he thrust the thin, but strong, blade along the top of the drawer until the lock gave. Carefully, he went through the sheaf of papers he found there, holding them close to the lamp as he scanned through them. Most of them related to the time when Hank had been Sheriff, but he could find none that mentioned Jeff Carswell.

In another drawer, he came across several samples of ore, together with some bags of gold dust. These, he guessed, belonged to Ferris. He felt a rising anger in his mind. Clearly the deputy Sheriff was busy lining his own pocket at the expense of the ordinary, decent citizens of Twin Ranchos. It made him feel sick at the thought of a crooked lawman running the place, carrying out orders from higher up, and receiving money and gold for it. For the first time, he wondered vaguely whether it might not have been Ferris who had shot down his brother in cold blood. It would certainly have been a motive – getting this job; and it was just possible that Ferris had been working hand in glove with Carswell for some time and Hank had found out about it and threatened to expose him. Frightened, seeing his wealth slipping from his grasp, Ferris had plucked up the courage to shoot Hank down before the other had had a chance to go for his gun.

Certainly, whoever had killed Hank, had known just where to find him, had known where his room was. That meant it had been someone who knew him intimately, knew he would be in town that night. He grinned wryly as the last thought crossed his mind. Since he had ridden into town with the bodies of several of the Booth gang across their saddles, everybody in town would have known he had returned.

That idea might not lead him anywhere, he thought dryly. He forced the last drawer of the desk, stared down into it, found that it was empty. Brows puckered, he wondered why anyone had gone to the trouble to lock an empty drawer. Perhaps it had contained something of importance and it had been locked automatically when the important papers had been removed and placed elsewhere.

He sighed. It was beginning to look as if there was a wall safe somewhere in the office and the sooner he started looking for it, the better. Half an hour later, he was forced to admit to himself that he was beaten. He had examined every inch of the walls of the room and there was nothing. If a wall safe did exist in the office it had been hidden so well that he had been completely unable to locate it. There were no hollow patches around the walls which would have given an indication of a safe set into the wall, no hidden buttons which would cause a section of the wall to slide aside.

Baffled, he returned to the desk and sank down into the chair behind it, stretching his legs out straight in front of him, feeling the deep-seated weariness in his limbs, soak through him. He knew that he needed sleep, that pretty soon he would find it impossible even to think straight.

There was the sound of footsteps on the boardwalk outside the building, coming closer. Swiftly, he placed his hand around the glass top of the lamp, felt the heat burn through to his flesh, but it had cut down the light so that it would be difficult for anyone to see any showing through the door or shuttered windows into the street outside. The footsteps came level with the outer door, seemed to hesitate, then continued on, fading into the distance. He drew in a deep breath and let it go in slow, small pinches of sound. His heart had jumped, thumping against his ribs and he could feel the tension beginning to heighten and drag on him.

Evidently, there were still people awake and abroad in the town. He sat back in the chair, trying to figure things out so that they would make some kind of sense for him. At the moment, he was utterly baffled. He had felt sure there would be something here in this office that would give him a lead on Hank's killer. Now that he had been through the room and found nothing, the sense of letdown felt strong within him, dampening his spirit. He sat loose in all of his joints, staring straight in front of him. It seemed incredible that he could have been so mistaken. Maybe the information he was looking for had been gathered by Hank, and Ferris had been more clever than he had reckoned and had destroyed it as soon as he discovered it. It seemed likely that Hank had not known of Ferris's double-crossing actions in the town when he had made the other his deputy. Could be that he had also trusted the man with the information that Carswell was mixed up in the rustling of other ranchers' cattle and once Hank was out of the way, Ferris had known exactly where to go for that information. The feeling of defeat washed over him strongly as he sat there in the dim yellow light of the lamp, thinking his black thoughts.

He felt burnt out and useless. That killing of Booth had also affected him, he told himself. He had felt sure that by destroying the outlaw, he had killed the man most likely to have murdered Hank. Yet that had clearly not been the way of it at all. Sighing deeply, he leaned his elbows on the desk, rubbed absently at the muscles at the nape of his neck, trying to think things out clearly. Shifting his position a little his right knee struck the edge of the drawer sharply, sending a stab of pain through his leg.

Glancing down, a sudden thought came to him. Taking

the lamp from the top of the desk, he shone the light into the drawer, not quite sure of what he was searching for. The drawer seemed empty. He pulled it out as far as it would go, noticed that unlike the others it was impossible to pull it completely from the desk. Bending, his probed with his fingers along the inside, felt the catch at one side and pressed it carefully. There was a slight movement and then the back of the drawer slid forward, hinged at the bottom.

So that was it! No wonder the drawer had been left deliberately empty, so that anyone might give it no more than a cursory glance and not think of investigating it further. There was only a small space at the back of the drawer, but his fingers touched papers and carefully he pulled them out, spread them on the desk in front of him, setting the lamp back so that he could read them clearly.

Ten minutes later, he knew that he had been on the right trail all the time. These papers were sufficient to incriminate Carswell up to the neck. Evidently, Hank had not been idle whenever complaints from the smaller ranchers had been filed with him. Here and there, he came across papers, signed by the county judge, instructing Carswell to remove his cattle from one or other of the ranches within seven days. He could imagine how Carswell must have hated Hank for this. He must have been used to having a lawman around town who did just as he was told who ignored the complaints of the other ranchers, giving Carswell the upper hand. But Hank had been straight and honest, had carried out the law as he saw it, with no fear of any man.

Thrusting the papers back into the drawer, he relocked the secret compartment at the back. He guessed that Ferris had not discovered this partition and the papers behind it, otherwise he would have informed Carswell and they would have been destroyed by now, once they knew he was in town looking for his brother's killer. Maybe, after all, Hank had not trusted Ferris all that much. The papers would be safe there until he needed them again; safer than carrying them on his person. Ferris would know that the desk had been broken into because of the forced locks on the drawers, but he would feel reasonably confident that whoever had done it, had found nothing of importance there.

Blowing out the lamp, he moved catlike towards the rear door. Moments later, he had crawled back through the low window at the rear of the building and was standing in the alley with the cold night air blowing about him, rustling among the boxes and litter at his feet. He was deep in thought as he made his way down the alley to where he had left his horse. He could just make it out, a few yards away, standing where he had tethered it. Behind him, in the main street, there were a few hoarse yells as the cowboys started coming out of the saloons. Judging by the moon, he reckoned it to be a little after midnight. Pretty soon, the town would be quiet until morning.

Feeling his way along the side of the broken wall, he turned over in his mind the various possibilities which had now been opened up for him following what he now knew. He could ride out and face Carswell with this information, note the other's reactions to it, but after a moment's debate he turned down that idea. Carswell would be a tough proposition on his own range, with his men around him.

Moving forward, he reached his mount, caught hold of the bridle to pull himself up into the saddle and at that same moment, heard the soft step at his back. He whirled swiftly, sensing the man directly behind him, grabbing for his sixgun as he turned, pivoting on one heel. The weapon was scarcely half-drawn when something hard and heavy crashed down on the side of his head and he pitched to his knees, strove desperately to retain a hold on his buckling consciousness, but failed and dropped forward into a deep and wide sea of utter blackness.

Much later, fog blurring his eyes and his head ringing with a throbbing ache, he came shuddering back to consciousness, realized that somebody had dragged him out of the alley and that he was inside a building of some kind. He blinked open his eyes and tried to focus them on details around him, but it was still dark and he could see very little. Moving his head a little, he tried to get to his feet, realized that his hands and ankles were tied and that he had been pushed up against a wall. Wincing with pain, he noticed a dim lantern swinging from a wooden beam a few feet away, the circle of light under it moving in time with the swaying of the lamp, sometimes touching his outstretched feet and then swinging away, lighting up the side of the table five or six yards from where he lay. His muscles felt stiff and sore and there was the slickness of blood on the side of his head. Shaking his head in an attempt to clear it, he was gradually able to focus his eyes more clearly. Evidently he had been unconscious for some time, how long he did not know.

Then a voice said from out of the pool of darkness behind the glow of the lantern: 'So you're comin' round, Wellman. I figure it's about time. I didn't think I'd hit you so goddamned hard.'

Screwing up his eyes, Rod tried to place the man, then just made out the dim shadow at the far side of the table. There were two other men with him, he noticed and after a moment, he knew that it had been Ferris who had spoken.

Licking his lips, he said harshly: 'Just what sort of a joke is this, Ferris?'

'This is no joke. Wellman,' retorted the other. 'I guess I've got enough evidence to toss you into jail right now.' There was a note of sarcastic amusement in his voice as he went on: 'Seems you wanted to break into the jail badly enough. You lookin' for somethin' in there?'

'Then why don't you put me in jail?'

'We've got some questions to ask you first. Then I figure Ryan here wants to finish some business with you that's been on his mind for some time.'

'Ryan! I figured he would be in on this.' Rod screwed up his lips, flickered his glance towards the other men, just able to make out their features now. He saw the heavy-jowled gunman standing to the right of the other man, one he did not recognize. 'And who's this?' he asked shortly.

'The name is Carswell,' said the other gruffly. 'I hear that Julie Saunders has been talking to you. I can guess what it was she had to say, and to protect my own interests I decided to talk to you myself.'

'Did you have to get him to knock me over the head to do it?' said Rod bitterly.

Carswell smiled thinly, his teeth just showing in the dark shadow of his face. 'We spotted you riding into town and followed you. Seems you were interested in something inside the Sheriff's office, though what it was, we aren't sure – yet.'

'I figured Ferris might be there,' said Rod evenly. 'I wanted to have another talk with him about the critter who shot my brother.'

'Yes, your brother.' The rancher's tone was flat and devoid of any feeling. 'A tragic thing, but events like that are not uncommon in a growing territory such as this. He should have been guided by us, but instead he chose to see things differently.'

'So you had him killed to prevent any more trouble for yourself,' snapped Rod. He tried to ease the bonds around his wrists, but they had been tied too tightly for him to move them, and there was little feeling left in his hands.

'He wasn't killed on my orders, Wellman,' said the rancher tersely. 'But he was a man with plenty of enemies. Matt Booth was one of them so I hear. He broke up that bunch of outlaws in the hills the day before he was killed. Booth got away so I'm told. Why don't you try to find him and ask him whether he had anything to do with your brother's death.'

'I have asked him,' Rod said thinly. In the dimness, he saw the expressions on their faces change at that news, saw the quick look which Ferris flashed Carswell, the tightening of the rancher's lips.

'You've found Booth?' muttered the other, after a momentary pause. There was a veiled note of disbelief in his voice as he took a step forward, placing his knuckles on the table and resting his weight on his hands.

'That's right.' Rod turned towards Ferris. There was a tightness in his voice as he said: 'That ferret-faced *hombre* who was talking to you the first time I came into your office tried to kill me yesterday, shot at me from one of the alleys. Maybe he figured he'd succeeded, or that I'd be unconscious long enough for him to get away, but he left a clear trail out of town and I trailed him all the way into the hills. He led me straight to where Booth was holed up.'

'And where is Booth now?'

'Six feet under, along the trail out to the hills. He tried to shoot it out with me, but I got his horse and then holed him up among the rocks. He talked a lot before he died, assured me that he hadn't returned to town since that gunfight in the hills when his men were killed.'

Carswell laughed defensively. 'You surely don't believe the word of a killer like that. Sure he was the one who shot your brother.'

'I believe him, because he knew he was dying when he told me,' Rod said flatly. 'That's why I went to the Sheriff's office, hopin' to take Ferris here by surprise and force him to tell me some more about what happened that night.'

Ferris moved around the corner of the table, advanced on Rod. Without any warning, he lashed out with his boot, caught Rod on the shin, knocking him over on his side. Pain jarred redly through his leg and up into his body. He sucked in a sharp gust of air, biting down the cry of pain that rose unbidden to his lips.

Viciously, Ferris said: 'You seem to have been snoopin' around too much, Wellman. You're gettin' too dangerous to have around. Maybe we ought to finish you here and now.'

'Like you did my brother – so that you could get his job?'

'I didn't shoot your brother,' said the other tightly. 'But

I'm glad that he's dead. That do-gooder was foulin' up
every move we made.'

'That will do, Ferris,' snapped Carswell from the other
side of the table. His tone brooked no argument and
Ferris lapsed into a sullen silence.

From the other corner of the room, Ryan said: 'What
are you goin' to do with him, boss? Reckon he knows a lot
too much. He may have found out somethin' while he was
in the Sheriff's office. There's no tellin' what Hank
Wellman discovered while he was Sheriff.'

'Don't worry. This *hombre* is not goin' to tell anybody,
even if he did manage to discover anything.' There was a
note of finality in Carswell's voice.

'Don't forget that this *hombre* is mine,' said Ryan.

'I'm not forgettin'.' Carswell turned to the gunhawk:
'But I don't want it to happen here. Too close to home.
There might be some questions asked. At the moment, I
don't want to risk a showdown with the Triple Star. Once
the rest of the boys get back, we'll consider that. They've
stood in my way too long, but when I do run them off that
spread, I'll have all of the boys at my back.'

Ryan moved a step away from the table. His face was
tight and there was a feral glow at the back of his eyes. The
fingers of his right hand touched the butt of the gun in his
belt meaningly. 'I'll take him back along the trail a little
way and then let him have it,' he promised, 'and this time
I'll see to it that there's no slip-up.'

'You'd better,' said Carswell ominously, 'if you value
your job on the ranch. I want to be sure he won't make any
more trouble for us.'

Ryan came forward and pulled a knife from his belt,
clashing through the ropes around Rod's ankles. Then he
bent, caught him roughly by one arm and hauled him
savagely to his feet. Rod stood swaying for several
moments, unable to put out a hand to steady himself
against the wall. The blood rushed pounding to his head,
throbbing painfully at the back of his eyes. Ryan jabbed
the barrel of his sixgun into the small of Rod's back,

thrusting him forward. 'All right, Wellman, reckon we'd better get on with it. Your horse is outside. Don't try anythin' funny, or I'll kill you right now.'

There was an ominous click as Ryan drew back the hammer of his sixgun. Stumbling, Rod moved out of the door, found himself as he had half expected, back in the narrow alley. Evidently, he had been in one of the abandoned warehouses, well off the main street, where these men knew they would be safe from any interruptions. From the corner of his eye, he noticed Carswell and Ferris step away from the door, watch for a moment as Ryan forced him over to his horse, then they turned and walked quickly along the alley, side by side, without a backward glance.

Somehow, he managed to pull himself up into the saddle, where he sat swaying slightly as a feeling of nausea swept over him. He had lost his hat somewhere and the night air touched his face and neck with cold fingers, where sweat had formed on his flesh. Moving away, Ryan led his own horse out of the dark shadows, climbed into the saddle and motioned Rod forward.

'We'll ride out of town a little way,' he said darkly. 'Don't worry, I won't keep you long. Once we're away from here, it will be the end for you. I've been waiting for this a long time. But I never expected you to walk into a trap as simply as that. I told Ferris and Carswell you were too clever a man to be caught so easily. Seems I'd overestimated you.'

Rod let the other ramble on, knowing that so long as he was talking, the other was not watching him too closely in the darkness. There was his knife in the back of his belt and although they had taken away his guns, they had not bothered to search any further. If only he could slide it out of its leather sheath and thrust the handle into the back of the saddle, there was a possibility that he could cut the thongs around his wrists without the other seeing him.

They rode slowly through the narrow, deserted alleys, Ryan sometimes crowding near him and at others staying

well away. It was the work of several moments to slide the
sharp-bladed knife from its sheath and even then, he
almost dropped it as his fingers caught at it numbly.
Gritting his teeth, he tried to thrust it, handle-first, into
the back of the saddle. Unable to move his hands and
fingers more than an inch or so, he made several attempts
before the knife handle finally stuck in the leather.

Letting the air go from his lungs in small pinches, he
forced himself to relax. Ryan was riding alongside him
now as they approached the edge of town. Ahead of them,
the trail went out into the dark countryside, where the
shadows were long in the moonlight.

'You seem to have little to say for yourself now,
Wellman,' said Ryan gloatingly. 'Last time we met, you had
the whip hand. How do you like it when the position is
reversed.'

'You talk too much,' Rod said evenly.

Ryan whirled in his saddle. For a moment his hand
hovered above the butt of his gun, then he relaxed with a
harsh laugh. 'You're tryin' to get me riled, Wellman,' he
said tautly, 'but it ain't goin' to work. I've already picked
out the spot where I intend to finish you. And when it's
done, there'll be nothin' to connect us with your death.'

Pressing his lips tightly together, forcing himself to
ignore the pain as the sharp blade of the knife touched his
wrists, nicking the flesh until the blood was flowing freely
down them, he sawed away at the ropes. The knife was
sharp, honed to a razor-edge and slowly, the strands of the
rope parted one by one. Fifteen minutes after he had
begun sawing at them, his hands were free. He continued
to sit upright in the saddle, flexing his fingers, fightng to
bring feeling back into them. He watched Ryan out of the
corner of his eye, knew that the other was confident that
nothing could possibly go wrong this time and it was going
to be this feeling of over-confidence which would lead to
his downfall.

The trail curved away ahead of them, leading north so
that the moon was behind them. Less than half a mile

away, Rod saw the looming hulk of dark hills, guessed that it would be here Ryan intended to kill him. As they drew closer to the hills, his eyes made out the narrow crevasse which slashed across the ground, standing out clearly in the moonlight. Rough bushes and grass grew on the top of it and from where he was, he could make out the stunted trees that grew out from the steep sides. He reckoned it was perhaps two hundred feet deep, a sheer drop through the branches of the trees onto the rocks below. Suddenly, he knew that it would be here that Ryan would kill him, dropping his body into that ravine where only the buzzards and the coyotes would find it. Nobody would come looking for him there and these men could feel reasonably safe that nobody would be able to tie them in with his disappearance.

He ran his tongue over dry lips, moved his fingers a little more, then gently eased the knife from the back of the saddle with his right hand, taking care not to move any more than was absolutely necessary. Ryan still rode ahead, his face tight and grim in the moonlight. He seemed very sure of himself. As they drew near to the edge of the ravine, the gunhawk reined up his mount, turned slowly in the saddle, lips twisted into a bestial grin.

'I reckon this will be as good a place as any, Wellman,' he said shortly.

SIX

Death in the Moonlight

'Seems to me you always make sure that you have a gun on your opponent, when you make a play like this,' Rod said evenly. 'I heard you were a gunfighter, but I now know you're a yeller-livered coward like so many more of your kind. Hand me a gun and we'll do this thing right.'

Ryan grinned and shook his head slowly. 'I saw you pull your own gun back in that saloon in Hatchet Bend, Wellman,' he retorted, 'and I know I wouldn't clear leather facing you down. No, I prefer to do things this way, it's a lot safer as far as I'm concerned. Besides, I want to be sure of this.'

Except for a faintly throbbing head, Rod no longer felt any effects of the blow from Ferris's gun. 'So you intend to shoot me down in cold blood, Ryan?'

'That's right,' grinned the other. He eased himself round in the saddle, touched the butt of his sixgun.

'You're callin' the play, Ryan,' Rod said evenly. 'But at least, you might do one thing for me.'

The gunman snapped harshly: 'What is it you want, Wellman?'

'You could tell me whether you were the coyote who shot my brother.'

Ryan laughed harshly. Then he shrugged his shoulders. 'I had no love for that Sheriff, but I didn't kill him. I know that Carswell wanted him out of the way and maybe we would have taken care of him. But it seems that somebody got to him before we did and saved us a heap of trouble.'

Rod narrowed his eyes. Once again, he had the feeling that this man was telling the truth as Booth had been. Every lead he had had seemed to take him nowhere. He had ridden a number of diverse trails, hoping to find the man who had pulled that trigger, yet every time he had come up against a blank wall. Whoever it had been, he was keeping low. It might have been Carswell, of course, or even Ferris.

'I guess that's all I can tell you.' Ryan's lips drew back in a mirthless smile. 'At least you can go down into hell not knowing who shot your brother. Still, it could be that you'll be able to ask him yourself in a little while.' Still grinning viciously, he closed his fingers around the gun, drew it gently from its holster. It was still poised there, just clear of leather, when Rod's arm moved. He saw the startled look of sudden realisation on the gunhawk's face, as his arm flashed up and down, the blade of the knife glinting bluely in the moonlight. Desperately, Ryan dug spurs into his mount, tried to bring up the barrel of the gun, finger tightening on the trigger.

Then he swayed in the saddle, the gun tilting from his fingers, dropping to the ground as he stared down in stunned, shocked surprise at the knife, buried to the hilt in his chest. He put up his left hand, fingers touching the hilt of the knife as if trying to draw it out of his body. There was a widening stain of red on his shirt. Lifting his head, he stared across at Rod, lips moving as he tried to mouth words, but no sound came. For a moment, he remained in the saddle. Then a gush of blood spilled from his mouth and he fell sideways from the saddle, hitting the ground hard like a sack of flour as his horse reared up, then bolted back down the trail.

Slipping from the saddle, Rod went over to the other, withdrew the knife and wiped the blade on the gunhawk's shirt before slipping it back into his belt. His own wrists were still bleeding a little and a moment later, when he found a small stream that ran over smooth-white rocks, he bent and bathed them in the ice-cold water. It stung his flesh, but he gritted his teeth and washed all of the blood away, wiping them on his neckpiece.

Wind scoured the canyon slopes and its coldness was beginning to reach deep into his bones as he went back to where Ryan lay, bent, caught the other up under the arms and pulled him to the lip of the ravine, then let him go, the outlaw's body plummeting and twisting as it crashed down the rocky face, snapping the out-thrusting branches on the way down. Going back to the other's horse, which had halted fifty yards away, he slapped it hard on the rump, watched as it galloped off into the moonlight. His face felt sticky with sweat and he wiped it away with his sleeve, tasting the salt on his lips.

In the moonlight he made out the white scar of the trail in front of him, noticed that in places, where it wound around the top of the crevasse, it had fallen away, that fresh slides had tumbled a lot of it into the ravine. Knowing it would be dangerous to ride that way, he led his horse downward, taking every step with caution. Hunger rumbled in his belly and he felt tired and bruised. In places, there was only just enough room for himself on the narrow trail and he edged forward carefully, leading the animal on, halting patiently whenever the horse jerked its head up sharply, halting, trembling a little. Coaxing it, he finally made it to the other side of the ravine.

Suddenly, he was aware of the fact that he had no guns in his belt, and cursed himself for not having taken Ryan's when he had killed him. There was no time to ride back now. He set his face in the direction of the Triple Star ranch, leaning forward a little in the saddle as he fought to combat the weakness in his body. Blended with the tiredness was a nausea that ate through his stomach, made his head swim. The blow on the side of the head seemed to have affected him more than he had realised at first. Gingerly, he put up his hand and touched it, felt it raw and open and it was still bleeding a little.

The trail led him on through loose gravel and rough-hewn boulders, etched and roughened by long ages of wind and rain. Part of the way he rode along the bank of a river, shining faintly in the flooding moonlight, the surface covered by a thin glow, sparkling when the under-tow rippled it over the jagged rocks. Half a mile along the river, he stopped and studied his situation, peering about him. The river made a slow, winding curve through the dark country that stretched away in front of him and across it, a rough shoulder of ground came right down to the very edge and he guessed there was no sure way to ford it there. He put his mount through the rough grass and brush which bordered it on his side and a little while later, came to a wrinkle in the ground, lifting fifty feet or more towards a long ridge. It was a rough slope, particularly in the moonlight which made shadows treacherous and diffi-cult to assess, but it was a passable one once he got the horse along it and presently he was riding along the ridge, gaining the shelter of tall pines before coming out onto the plain that skirted the perimeter of the Triple Star ranch.

He rode openly here, for the moon was going down in the west, leaving the sky dark ahead of the dawn and he knew it was distinctly possible Julie Saunders still had men watching the trail and if he tried to get in unobtrusively, they might mistake him for one of Carswell's men and he could catch a bullet before he was aware of his danger.

Fighting his way over some of the roughest footing he had known, having to dismount in places and lead his horse, he came finally to pasture land and made better time, eventually coming onto the slope of one of the three hills that looked down on the ranch. By now, it was almost dawn with a faint grey bar lying across the distant horizon, picking out the undulating crests of the hills in that direction.

The ranch was in complete darkness as he rode down the slope and into the courtyard, reining his horse near the gate of the corral, but even as he was dismounting and putting his horse into the corral, a light came on in one of the windows. Closing the gate, he walked wearily across the courtyard, his spurs scuffing up the dust underfoot. There was a moment's silence and then the ranch door opened and he saw the girl framed in the opening, the light of a lantern behind her, outlining her figure with a pale yellow radiance.

'Who is it?' she called. There was no fear in her voice, merely a note of curiosity. Possibly, he thought, she guessed it was one of the hands having ridden in from the camp.

'Rod Wellman,' he called back, stepping forward where he was clearly visible to her.

'Come inside,' she said quietly. She stood on one side so that he might enter and then closed the door behind her. She had a robe wrapped tightly around her and her long hair was done in plaits hanging down over her shoulders. She gave a little gasp as she caught sight of the blood on the side of his face.

'What happened? You've been in a fight.'

Somehow, he managed to grin, but it cost him an effort to do so. Now that most of the excitement was past, his mind was able to dwell on his own physical condition and the pain was beginning to make itself felt.

He nodded his head, sank down in the chair at the table while the girl placed the lantern down and came over to him, concern showing on her delicate features. 'Carswell and that gunhawk of his, Ryan, tried to finish me permanently,' he explained. 'I went along to Ferris's office to look around for something which might tell me who had killed Hank. They must have seen me ridin' into town because they were waitin' for me when I got out of the building, knocked me on the head and tied me up in one of the abandoned warehouses.'

'Was Jeff Carswell with them?' asked the girl, as she made him hold his head on one side so that she might examine the gaping wound at the side of his temple.

'Yes, he was there.'

'I thought he might be,' said the girl bitterly. 'He no doubt came to make sure that his orders were carried out and nothing went wrong this time. He's worried in case the ordinary townsfolk find out that he's running the town and decide to take the law into their own hands.'

'You could be right.' Rod winced as the girl probed the wound, tightening his lips momentarily into a hard line. 'He did mention that he doesn't want a showdown with the Triple Star ranch at the moment, not until the rest of his men get back. Then he means to attack you.'

'He must have been quite certain that you wouldn't be alive to tell me that.'

'He was. He gave Ryan orders to ride me out of town and kill me. He didn't want to do it close to town just in case my death was connected with him.'

'What happened that made it possible for you to escape?' The girl went over to the other side of the room, came back with a box containing bandages and a pair of scissors. 'This is going to hurt a little,' she warned, smiling down at him seriously, 'but it's got to be done. I shall have to clean that wound before I bandage it.'

He nodded, watched as she brought over a basin of hot water and a cloth. As she began bathing it, cleansing it with gentle movements, he said: 'Ryan must have taken both of my guns, but he wasn't too thorough when he searched me, because he left me with my knife. I managed to get it out and push it into the back of the saddle as we rode out of town and cut the ropes around my wrists. When he stopped along the trail, he got careless, figuring there was nothing I could do.'

'So you killed him?'

Rod nodded. 'Had to. It was either him or me. I got

him with the knife. It was more of a chance than he would have given me.'

She nodded in agreement. Binding the bandage around his head, she stepped back to review her handiwork. 'That should do,' she said, smiling down at him. 'How does it feel?'

'Fine,' he said.

Replacing the box in the drawer, she came back, stood for a moment beside his chair, then said: 'I'll get something to eat and then you can sleep for a while. You look as if you haven't slept properly for days.'

'What do you intend to do about Carswell?' He gave her a bright-sharp stare. 'He'll ride in and finish you as soon as he gets all of his men together.'

'I know.' Her face was serious as she stood there, with the lamplight etching it with shadow. 'We'll hit him first. This may sound hard, but it's the only way. My father fought for this ranch ever since he built it, mostly with his own hands, and when he died, I swore that I would carry on his work no matter what happened. I mean to keep my word. Carswell will have to be stopped. They're an evil lot of men and nobody will be safe until we've finished them all.'

'Have you got enough men to do it?'

Julie stared at him, for the moment revealing nothing. Then she said with a break of confidence in her voice: 'I've got enough.'

'I'll help if you need me.'

'I'll need every gun I can get, but we'll finish them.' She turned and went into the kitchen. Rod sat back in his chair, feeling the weariness flood over him. His head still ached a little but the feeling of nausea had faded and the room was no longer spinning around him. He was not sure how many men the girl could call upon when it came to a showdown with Jeff Carswell. She had told him earlier that it was not easy to keep men here at the Triple Star spread and he had guessed then that this had probably been due to the fact that Carswell and his bunch frightened them off. If that was the case, how many of the men she had now would ride against Carswell? He knew it was a question that could not be answered until the time came and put it out of his mind. From the way Carswell had been speaking, it would be some little time before his men were up to their full strength. They had to hit him before then.

He ate ravenously when the meal was placed in front of him, finished with the coffee, drinking it down rapidly, hot as it was. Some of the warmth came back into his spent body and only the deep-seated weariness remained. When the meal was finished, Julie said quietly: 'There's a bed through there. Better get as much sleep as you can. After breakfast, I'll call the boys together and talk this thing over with them. There has to be a way of stopping Carswell.'

'Be careful how you put that proposition to 'em,' Rod said warningly, 'they may decide that to go up against Carswell and his bunch of hired killers, isn't too healthy, even though there may be only half of them at the ranch. If your own men ride over the hill and leave you, rather than take the trail against Carswell, you could be finished.'

'I think I know how to handle them,' Julie said confidently. 'With men like these you have only to scorn them into shame and they'll ride. They hate to be looked upon as cowards by a woman.'

'Maybe.' Rod's tone was non-committal. He followed her out of the room, down a short corridor. She moved her head towards the open door of a room. 'In here,' she said.

It was a bedroom with the iron bed close against the far wall. 'I'll call you around noon,' Julie said, stepping back into the corridor.

He turned to thank her, but she had already gone. He heard her footsteps fading along the corridor. Then he closed the door, went over to the window and looked out, on to the green pasture at the side of the ranch. The dawn was brightening now and he could make out the smooth line of the hills on the skyline and the pale blue of the sky over them. Undressing, he lay down on the bed and pulled the cool sheets over him. It was good to be able to stretch out, to surrender oneself to the overpowering sense of weakness and tiredness that was suffused throughout his body, not to have to think of anything. He felt as if he were sinking into the sheets, his body buoyed up by some unseen force. Then sleep came and he did not waken until someone touched his shoulder, bringing him instantly awake with an animal-like alertness to danger. He relaxed at once as he saw Julie smiling down at him.

'I let you sleep as long as I could,' she said. 'There's a bowl of soup I made for you.'

'Thanks.' He pushed himself up into a sitting position. Julie left the room and he swung his feet to the floor, stood up, swaying a little, touching the bandage around his scalp gingerly. The pain in his head was almost gone now and the sleep had given him a new strength. The soup was hot and he did not pause until he had finished every drop.

In the parlour, be found the girl seated at the window, looking out over the courtyard and corral with a certain wistfulness to her features. She turned quickly as he walked into the room. For a moment, as he stood there, he saw that her guard was down, that she no longer looked so supremely confident that everything was going to turn out all right. She looked just like a little girl who had suddenly been faced with a problem far too big for her even to understand. She looked defenceless and not a little fright-ened.

He saw her struggle bravely as she felt his piercing gaze on her and forced a quick smile. Getting to her feet, she said quietly: 'I've been talking with some of the men. They don't like the idea of riding against Carswell. They think that maybe you picked up the story wrongly and that they'll be riding straight into a trap if they go.'

'I suppose they would make an excuse like that,' Rod said tightly. He hitched the gunbelt more tightly around his middle, felt the empty holsters there and said softly: 'Do you think you could fix me up with a couple of Colts.

Then I'll go out and have a talk with these men of yours.'

'Do you think they'll listen to you when they wouldn't to me?' she asked. She went across to the desk near the window, unlocked one of the drawers and brought out a pair of revolvers which she placed on top of the desk. 'These were my father's,' she went on, without waiting for him to answer her earlier question. 'Somehow, I think he would have wanted you to wear them if he had known you. He liked your brother, always said that he was the only proper Sheriff that Twin Ranchos ever had.'

'I think I'd have liked to have known your father,' Rod said simply. He picked up the guns, fed bullets into the chambers, spun them automatically, liking the feel, the balance, of the weapons. Then he thrust them into the holsters. 'Where are these men of yours, Julie?'

'You'll find them over at the bunkhouse,' she said. 'Do you mind if I come over with you?'

He shrugged. 'Suit yourself. Things might get a little heated before I'm through with them.'

When he stepped inside the bunkhouse, he saw several men, some seated at the table playing cards, others lying on their bunks. They eyed him indifferently as he walked in, with the girl at his back, then got slowly to their feet as Julie said with a touch of sharpness to her tone:

'This is Rod Wellman, boys. Hank Wellman's brother. He's got something to say to you.'

Rod eyed them closely, feeling their eyes on him. They were mainly of the same breed, he thought, letting his gaze wander over their faces, men who feared or distrusted a stranger.

'You all know that Carswell has sworn to finish this ranch,' Rod began, his voice serious, harsh. 'He thought that he had finished me a little while ago, and he said then that he has men riding up to join him in a little while, but that he doesn't want any trouble yet because he knows he'll lose out on the deal. We've got to hit him now, before he's ready, and hit him hard.' He paused deliberately and then said harshly: 'I hear that you're all scared to face up to him.'

'We've got no objections fighting Carswell, but how do we know you're tellin' the truth,' said one of the men harshly. He took a step forward, a big hulking brute of a man, arms swinging loosely at his sides. 'Could be that you picked him up wrong. Seems unlikely to me that he'd say a thing like that in front of you if he knew there was any chance of you warnin' us about it.'

'I told you,' Rod said evenly. 'He had me at the wrong end of a gun, felt sure I'd never live to tell anybody about it. But as you see, I am here and —'

'And how do we know you ain't in cahoots with Carswell, tellin' us this just to have us ride out and be shot to pieces?' There was a deliberate sneer in the other's voice. He thrust his face close to Rod's, lips twisted. 'Seems to me that you've done a lot of talking, but you ain't convinced me that we ought to ride out there and try to take the Carswell bunch.'

'You talk too much,' Rod said thinly. He eyed the other directly. He felt the quick heat in his face, then forced it down.

For a moment, the man stared at him. Then he sidled forward, said thickly: 'Nobody talks to me like that, mister.'

The other was a solid shape, his features burned almost black by the weather, eyes set close together against his squat nose; a man hungering for a fight, determined that he was not going to be spoken to by this stranger who had come pushing into the ranch, worming his way into the girl's confidence with his talk of riding against Carswell.

Rod had seen many like him along the trail. Hard men, governed more by passion than by reason, believing that every problem could be resolved by their fists or a gun, restless men, narrow of mind. He saw the shine in the other's eyes, the tight twist of his mouth.

Squaring himself at Rod, the man went on slowly, mouthing the words: 'You seem to know everythin' about Carswell. Suppose you ride out against him see how far you get with —' He never completed his sentence. It had been meant only as a feint for what he really intended to do. Without any warning, he swung up a ham-like fist, meaning to connect with the point of Rod's chin, but talk on the part of a man like this was an old trick when it came to a fist fight and Rod had guessed what he meant to do even before he swung with his fist. Sidestepping the blow neatly, Rod allowed it to roll along his arm, then whipped in a solid right to the man's chest. The other grunted and gave ground as the blow shook him up a little. He narrowed his eyes to mere slits, tightened his lips into a hard line and came in again, boring forward, face murderous. Lowering his head and shoulders suddenly, he lunged forward, wrapping his fingers together behind the small of Rod's back, and squeezing tightly as he could, striving to lift the other off his feet, so that he could apply more pressure and snap Rod's spine.

But he made the mistake of not thrusting his head forward into Rod's chest as he strove to swing him off balance. Swiftly, Rod brought up his right hand, shoved the heel of it under the other's chin and heaved with all his strength. Eyes glaring, the other's head was forced back on his shoulders, exposing his neck. Slowly, the man was forced to loosen his hold around Rod's middle and before he could regain his balance, Rod had slashed up with the side of his stiffened hand, hitting the man across the windpipe with a savage, chopping blow. Gagging, struggling to draw air down into his lungs, his neck muscles paralysed by the force of that blow, the man fell back. His eyes popped in his head and his tongue thrust itself from his mouth like a man dangling on the end of a tightening, strangling rope.

Rod let him stand there for a long moment, then swung a vicious haymaker almost from the floor, catching the man flush on the point of the chin. His eyes glazed over even before he had hit the floor of the bunkhouse. Knocked out by the stunning force of the blow, he lay where he had fallen. Rod stood away from him, turned to face the rest of the men, standing around in a wide circle, amazement written over their coarse features. Clearly they had never considered the possibility that this hulking giant of a man would lose the fight which had seemed so uneven to them at the beginning. The fight had half-broken Rod's restraint and he said harshly, speaking through tightly-clenched teeth: 'Does anybody else want the same, or are you goin' to listen to me?'

Behind him, he heard the girl say quietly: 'I think they've learned the lesson, Rod.'

One of the men, his hair greying at the temples, stepped hesitantly forward, said softly: 'You positive about Carswell being short of men at the moment, Wellman?'

Rod nodded. 'I'm sure,' he told them, 'if we ride out now, we can finish them for good and end this menace in the territory. Wait any longer and you may never get another chance.'

'We're with you,' murmured the other. He turned and shot a quick look at the rest of the men. 'All right boys, saddle up.'

'What about Clem?' asked one of the men, jerking his thumb at the man stretched out unconscious on the floor.

'Leave him,' snapped the other harshly. 'If he wants to follow us and be in at the finish then he can. But judging from the way you hit him, Wellman, I'd say he'll be out cold for some time.'

High noon and the heat shimmered on the trail, touched the rocks with fire, reflecting the sickening glare from all sides of the trail. They had left the green grass of the meadows and pastures behind shortly after riding out of the Triple Star ranch and now they were riding in a tight bunch through open, rocky ground with the edge of the alkali desert looming up in front of them. The trail skirted around the desert, cut up into the rocky escarpments that encroached on it, but Rod led them straight across the Badlands. It was the shortest route and the one which would not be watched by any of Carswell's men. He was not sure yet whether Carswell knew that he had escaped, that he was still alive, still a menace to them; a bigger menace than he might have ordinarily been now that he knew how short of men they were. It was possible that Carswell had attached no importance to the fact that Ryan had not yet ridden back from his chore. It was probable that Ryan rode off at times after killing a man on Carswell's orders and got himself drunk in the town. If that was the case, Carswell would not yet be worried about his non-appearance. But there was just the possibility that Carswell was expecting the gunhawk back right away and now he would have guessed that something had gone wrong and he would be taking no chances on being attacked by surprise.

Rod glanced at the girl who rode beside him. Julie Saunders had insisted on riding with them, maintaining that defending the ranch was as much her concern as that of the men, that if her father had been alive, he would have ridden with them and it was only right that she should do so. Rod had tried to argue with her, but to no avail and in the end he had been forced to allow her to come. It was not going to make things any easier for them, having her around, he told himself. Most of his time he would be concerned with seeing that nothing happened to her, instead of making sure that the Carswell men did not gain the upper hand.

The heat wrapped itself around them like a thick and impenetrable blanket, a wall of invisible shimmering that brought the sweat boiling out into their bodies. Rod felt his shirt sticking to his flesh, chafing and irritating and the bandage around his head, soaking up some of the perspiration was also beginning to itch intolerably. He had wanted to take it off, afraid that it would mark him out, even though he wore a hat that covered most of it from sight, but Julie had insisted that he keep it in place, warning him of the danger of infection in such a wound. He smiled wryly to himself. She seemed to have been making a lot of decisions, he reflected. A strong-minded girl, evidently ready to follow her father.

The horses slowed their pace as they made their way

across the alkali. The white, caustic dust clogged their hooves, ate deep into their legs. It lifted from the ground and hung in the air as a hazy cloud, getting into their faces and nostrils. Even though they pulled their neckpieces up over their mouths and noses, it still managed to work its way into their throats somehow, until they gagged on it, their heads lowered against the blinding, overpowering glare of sunlight on the desert. It shocked up at them from every side. It hung in dizzying waves all about them. In the distance, the dust devils danced and cavorted in whirling spirals of white as the wind caught at them, twisting them along in vagrant eddies.

It was bad country, thought Rod, riding with his eyes slitted against the glare and dust. Country which would probably never be fully tamed. No man could grow anything here, it was useless for beef. There was scarcely any water from one end of it to the other. At present, it merely formed a protective barrier for the ranches which bordered it. No man in his right senses would try to ride across it, when he could take the longer, but far pleasanter, route around it.

If Carswell was suspicious, he would have men out watching the hill trail, but the chances were he would never consider watching this one. The afternoon wore on and Rod made them push their horses as much as they dared. He did not relish the idea of attacking Carswell on his own land in the dark. They reached the far edge of the desert as the sun began its long slide towards the western horizon, began the climb into the hills, circling around so as to reach the Carswell spread from the east. Once again, Rod hoped to take Carswell by surprise with this manoeuvre. The logical direction of attack was from the northwest.

'Another half hour should do it,' said one of the men harshly. It was the first time anyone had spoken since they had ridden into the desert. Here the air was cooler and speaking was a little easier without the alkali clogging one's throat.

'You think he will be waiting for us?' asked the girl. She turned her head and eyed Rod carefully.

He shrugged. 'That's somethin' we won't know until we get there. He may be wonderin' why Ryan didn't come back and if he sent men out to look for him they may have found his body at the bottom of that ravine. If they've located him and got back with the news, he'll guess what has happened and he'll know we'll be attacking.'

'It won't be easy then, will it?'

'No,' he said slowly, 'it won't be easy. But at least, we'll be fighting on level terms. Another few days and he would have hit you with an overwhelming number of men. That would have been the end of you and the ranch.'

'I know.' She placed her lips close together, looking ahead of her, the slanting sunlight touching her face, making it seem sombre and troubled. He thought that she was inwardly regretting having decided to ride out with them, that she would have preferred to have stayed back at the ranch. Even that would not have been easy, he mused. Waiting there, not knowing what was happening, not knowing how many of her hands would be brought back to the ranch over the saddles of their horses, or if any of them would return. It was only a momentary thought, but it forced a faint chill on his mind.

They hit up into the hills, felt them close in on them, where they moved close to the trail, shouldering in on both sides. Then, topping a rise, they reined up their mounts, looking down on the ranch that lay below them.

SEVEN
Range War

'Over there,' Rod called, motioning to the men to spread out along the side of the hill. 'They may be waitin' for us so watch yourselves when you move in.'

'Don't seem to be anybody around down there,' muttered one of the men thickly. 'You don't figure they may have ridden out, leaving the place unguarded.'

'Ain't likely,' Rod told him 'They may not be expectin' trouble. But it won't take 'em long to settle down as soon as we start shootin'.'

He waited until the men were stretched out in a wide line, moving forward in a half circle, putting their horses at the slope, some with rifles drawn, the other men carrying their sixguns, ready to open up the minute something showed. They were halfway down the slope before anything happened near the ranch. Then a rifle barked, a slug tore into the ground a foot from Rod's horse. It reared up high into the air, kicking out with its forelegs at the sudden sound and he fought savagely to control it. Carswell's voice yelled from one of the windows of the ranchhouse: 'We can see you all, Wellman. I don't know how you managed to kill Ryan and get away, but if you don't back off, all of your men will be killed. I'm givin' you fair warnin' to ride back off my land.'

Rod grinned tightly. 'That means he's scared,' he called, raising his voice so that all of the men could hear. He had noticed how they had dropped from their saddles at the sudden shot, going down under cover, and shouted more to reassure them than anything else. 'He wouldn't have given us the chance to turn around and ride out of here if he didn't know that he doesn't have a chance against us. He's only playing for time.'

A volley of gunfire broke from the ranch as they began to move in. Out of the corner of his eye, Rod saw a group of the men with him, move around to cover the rear of the buildings and ensure that none of Carswell's men escaped that way. By now, the Triple Star men were firing from cover and bullets crashed and tore into the wooden walls of the ranch. There seemed to be a small group of men hiding in the bunkhouse, but the thin wooden walls of that building afforded no protection against rifle fire and a moment later, they tried to make a run for the house.

Crouching low, Rod lifted his Winchester, sighted on one of the running men, squeezed the trigger gently after taking up the slack and saw the man go down. As a second man tried to make it across the open stretch of the court-yard, he was hit several times, spun round and then fell across the legs of the first man to die.

The gunfire was terrible. It hammered against the ranch from all sides. The glass of the windows was smashed in several places and somewhere in the heart of the din a man let up a great shout, a sound that was lost almost at once as more lead flailed through the walls. Rod heard more men yell inside the house. Every muscle in him was so tight that his body began to ache intolerably. With a tremendous effort, he forced himself to relax. At the moment, they seemed to have the upper hand. In spite of the fact that Carswell had been expecting them, he had been forced onto the defensive right from the start and if they could only keep it that way, he would soon be finished.

Crawling forward, he motioned to the girl to move

back, out of range of the guns, saw her hesitate, then retreat towards the comparative shelter of the trees a short distance away, where most of the horses were tethered. Feeling a little easier in his mind now that she was out of danger for the time being, he wriggled through the rough grass that grew on the slope, fired at a man who came diving out of the door of the ranch, dropping onto his face and slithering towards the corral. The other ducked out of sight and Rod knew that his shot had missed. The volume of fire from the ranch was diminishing slowly. Some of this was undoubtedly due to the men having to reload, but he guessed that some of them had been killed or wounded during the initial volleys.

Grinning a little to himself, he pumped another six shots into the windows of the long, low-roofed building, aiming at any target that presented itself. There seemed to be little the defenders could do now, but crouch helplessly behind the windows, occasionally risking a quick glance outside to avoid being caught in a surprise attack.

Breathing heavily, Rod shifted his position, dropped down behind a rock as a bullet whined off the top of the boulder, screaming into the distance with the yell of tortured metal. Jerking his head back, he drew one of the sixguns, lowering the empty rifle to the ground beside him. In the same instant, there was a shrill, high-pitched scream of warning behind him. For a moment, he could not realize what had happened. Then he turned his head with a wrenching of neck muscles, started to his feet as he saw the girl running from the trees, pointing one hand in the direction of the long, low ridge which lay to their right. He dragged his attention from her, arrested by the urgency in her gesture, cursed as he saw the handful of men who came over the top of the ridge, yelling and firing from the hip as they ran.

The girl was still stumbling forward down the slope towards him, and he saw some of the running men turn, aim their sixguns in her direction. Shouting a harsh warning, he raced towards her, getting to her within a few seconds and pulling her down behind an outcrop of rock as bullets whined and kicked all about them. She was breathing heavily and there was a look of bewildered apprehension on her face as she gasped: 'I just spotted them crawling up to the top of the hills a few seconds ago. They must have been hiding out there until we started to move in.'

Rod nodded grimly. He had overlooked Carswell's natural cunning. Once the other had realized that with Ryan's death he could expect an attack on the ranch at any time, he had taken the precaution of sending a handful of his men out into the rocks in the distance, knowing that if they were not spotted, the Triple Star riders would launch their attack on the ranch without thinking of any trouble from their rear, believing that all the ranch hands were in the house or bunkhouse, ready to repel the assault. He cursed himself inwardly for not having considered this possibility before. Now he had led the men into a trap and they were coming under murderous fire from both sides.

Wriggling forward, he risked a quick look around the side of the boulder, motioning to the girl to keep her head down. A bullet cut a furrow in the dirt a few inches from his hiding place, but he had caught sight of the two men moving forward, converging on the rocks. Swiftly, he fired a couple of shots over the boulder. A bullet sang dangerously close to his cheek, but his sudden move had taken both by surprise and one of his slugs reached its target, sending one of the men reeling sideways as he clutched at his torn shoulder.

The other men who had come over the hills were moving in on the Triple Star riders facing the ranchhouse, sending a rain of bullets among them. Taken from the rear, they were exposed to this fire. A few of them had turned and were shooting up the line of the slope at the advancing men. The rest tried to get under cover to keep up their fire at the ranch and prevent the men there from sallying forth and joining in the attack. Once Carswell and the others managed to move out of the ranch and close in on them the battle would be as good as lost.

Gritting his teeth, Rod aimed and fired at the second man as he came leaping forward. The girl screamed thinly as the man reached the boulders and hurled himself towards them. Rod had chance to trigger off one shot before the man hit him, knocking him backward onto the hard ground. Savagely, Rod reached out and caught the man's wrist, forcing it back as the other tried to align the barrel of his gun on his chest, his face a mask of bestial triumph.

Slowly, the gun barrel twisted towards him, lining itself up on his heart and he could see the other leaning his weight on the trigger. With a desperate, superhuman strength, Rod managed to get one leg beneath him, thrusting up with it, hurling the man off him. They rolled for several yards out into the open, bullets whistling all about them. Kicking out with his foot, Rod caught the other in the groin, and as the man doubled up in sudden agony, beads of sweat popping out on his forehead, a thin scream of agony bursting from his lips, he caught at his wrist with both hands, bending it savagely, turning the other's gun on himself. The man drew back his lips as he tried to force Rod's hands away. He was breathing heavily, air gasping in and out of his throat. Slowly, inexorably, Rod turned the gun in the other's hand, then pulled sharply. With a savage explosion the gun went off as the man's finger automatically tightened on the trigger by his sudden move and the gunhawk fell back, his own bullet through his heart.

Drawing air down into his heaving lungs, Rod kneed himself away from the other's body, glanced quickly around him. The gunhawks were now crouched down in a line less than ten yards from where he lay and for the moment they seemed to be more concerned with shooting down on the Triple Star men than bothering with him. Crawling back to the rocks where the girl lay, he grabbed at his gun, checked the chambers and then commenced to

fire down the slope. Three of the gunslingers died with
bullets in their backs before they grew aware of this new
danger. Evidently they had left Rod to the other two men.

Coolly Rod continued to bring a merciless fire down on
the men directly in front of him, knowing that he could
safely leave the others inside the ranch-house to the rest of
the Triple Star men. Only one of the men who had come
racing over the crest of the hill hoping to take them in the
back, still seemed to be alive. He lay behind a pile of rocks,
hidden from Rod's fire, occasionally lifting himself and
sending a shot in Rod's direction. It was not going to be
easy to winkle him out of that position, Rod reflected.
Glancing about him, he slid forward into the grass, keeping his head and shoulders down. So long as he did not lift
himself, he was out of sight of the other.

Carefully, he wormed his way forward an inch at a time.
The thunderous roar of the gunfight drowned out any of
the slight rustling noises his boots made as he edged
forward through the grass, working his way around the
rocks where the other lay hidden. Parting the grass, he
made out the shape of the man lying in a shallow depression in the ground. The other caught sight of the slight
movement at the same moment, whipped up his gun and
fired. The bullet scorched past Rod's cheek. An inch the
other way and it would have been through his brain. But
the gunman had no chance to fire a second shot; before
his finger could tighten again on the trigger, Rod had
lifted his own gun and fired. The gunhawk reeled back as
the bullet took him in the face. His arms pawed at the
empty air for a moment in an effort to maintain his
balance. Then he pitched forward onto his knees, over-
balanced the whole way and died.

Letting the breath rush through his parted lips, Rod
eased himself slowly to his feet, turned at a sudden swift
movement off to one side. One of the enemy was still on
his feet. The man he had shot and hit in the shoulder. The
other let out a sudden yell and fired. The bullet struck
Rod's gun and sent it whirling from his hand. He knew he

did not have the chance to draw the other before the man pressed the trigger for a second time; and that this time, the other would make no mistake. He saw the man draw back his lips into a thin line, grinning viciously. There was blood on his shirt where Rod's earlier bullet had taken him in the shoulder and he was swaying slightly on his feet, eyes clouded with pain, but he felt confident that he had this man at a disadvantage now, that he had only to fire and it would be finished as far as Rod Wellman was concerned.

Rod knew he hadn't a chance, but he also knew that he would have to make a try. He could see the man's knuckles whiten as he began to squeeze on the trigger. His left hand struck downward for the gun at his belt, his fingers just touched it when the sharp report of the gunshot came to his ears. In spite of himself he winced, expecting to feel the leaden impact of the bullet as it tore its way through his flesh, cutting through bone and muscle into his chest.

Then he realized that the gunman facing him was teetering on his feet, his arm dropping loosely to his side. The man managed to squeeze off one shot but it blasted harmlessly into the dirt at his feet as he stumbled, struggled to regain his balance, then collapsed limply onto his face in the dirt.

Slowly, Rod stared about him. Julie Saunders was on her feet near the rocks where he had left her, holding the smoking Colt in her right hand. Her face was ashen as she stumbled towards him, her lower lip quivering a little. 'I thought he would kill you,' she said, her voice quavering a little as she spoke. 'I didn't think I could hit him in time. Is he—?'

'He'd dead,' Rod said quietly. For a moment, he placed his arms around her, knowing the thoughts which were racing through her mind at that moment. It was always hard, killing one's first man and for her it would be even worse.

Down below, the firing around the ranch had risen in volume until it was a terrible thunder that hammered at the ears, the echoes reverberating from the hills on each side, adding to the din. Slowly, carefully, he made his way down to where the men were crouched in a half circle around the buildings. In a lull in the firing, he called loudly:

'Can you hear me, Carswell?'

There was a brief, uneasy pause, then the rancher's voice called harshly from one of the windows. 'I can hear you, Wellman. What's on your mind?'

'Better surrender now before there's any more killing. Those men you had planted to take us from the rear. They're all dead now and they can't help you. You're finished.'

'That's what you think, Wellman,' snarled the other. 'If you think that, why don't you come in and take me?'

'Don't be a fool. This way you get nothing. There's plenty of evidence back in town inside the Sheriff's desk to say that you were behind the rustling of those herds a few years back. Even Ferris is not goin' to be able to help you now. Either you die there, or we take you back into town to stand trial. The choice is yours.'

'Then here's your answer,' called the other. He punctuated his remark with a rifle shot. The bullet struck wide of Rod's position and whined off into the trees.

'All right. If that's the way you want it.' Rod paused, bit his lower lip, then called out. 'Any of you men in there who don't feel like dyin' for Carswell, come along out with your hands lifted.'

For a long moment, there was no answer. Then a man yelled: 'Hold your fire, Wellman, I'm coming out.' The voice came from the side of the house and a moment later, Rod saw the man step out into the courtyard there, his hands lifted over his head.

'All right,' he shouted. 'Step on up here and don't try any tricks.'

Keeping his hands raised, the man moved forward, not once turning his head to look behind him. Rod heard Carswell's sharp curse as the man stepped around the side of the house. 'Goddamn you, Flint. You ain't walkin' out on me like that, you coward.' There was the sharp bark of a Winchester. The man in the courtyard staggered as the slug took him in the back. For a moment, he remained upright, his eyes turned up towards the hill in front of him. Then his hands fluttered up for a moment as if trying to reach for something in the air just above his head. He half turned as if to face Carswell down, to stare at the man who had deliberately shot him in the back rather than allow him to surrender. Then, slowly, he staggered forward a couple of paces, reached the horse trough and slumped over it, his head splashing into the water.

'Nobody runs out on me,' Carswell yelled harshly. It was a warning to the rest of the men in the house with him. Rod sighed. Evidently the other would not surrender so long as he had any ammunition.

Lifting himself a little, Rod waved his men forward. Getting to his feet, he ran full tilt down the slope, waiting for a bullet to pick him out, aware that he was making an excellent target for the defenders in the ranch-house. Bobbing and weaving from side to side, he ran on, even when a volley of fire crashed out from the windows of the ranch. Then he was close enough to have to worry only about the fire from one side of the building, the corner of the ranch-house itself sheltering him from the other windows.

A bullet plucked at the sleeve of his jacket as he ran, the breath rasping in his throat. Then he had reached the wall of the building. Pressing himself close against it, he was safe for the moment. None of the men inside the room could fire at him without exposing themselves to his guns.

Standing there, he listened for any movement inside the room, for the sound of boots on the wooden floor, the rattle of sixguns against the wall, the harsh breathing of men crouched down under the ledge of the window. But he heard nothing.

Between the firing, the running, the crouching, and the waiting, he had scarcely given any thought as to what he could do now that he had reached the house. Somehow, he had to get inside, take Carswell by surprise. He still wanted the rancher alive, had the feeling that even if Carswell had not been behind his brother's death, the rancher knew who had done it. Once he got him back into town, he felt reasonably certain that he could get him to talk.

Cautiously, he eased his way along the wall in the direction of the bullet-smashed window. Inside, there was a sudden movement and a second later, he saw the hand holding the revolver, clearly framed in the opening. The man was wary, had probably seen the men who had dashed forward out of the cover of the grass and hurled themselves in the direction of the house, and the other did not intend to show himself or open fire until he knew where the men had gone. Rod stood there, quite still, gripping his guns, and waited.

Inch by inch, the man edged forward. A few moments later, Rod saw the brim of his hat appear, then the side of his head. Acting on impulse, he thrust the guns back into their holster, stood poised until the man eased his shoulders forward, and then moved swiftly, catching hold of the other by the front of his shirt, jerking him out of the window. The man uttered a high-pitched yell of surprise and fear as he hit the ground. His gun dropped from his fingers and before he could regain his balance, Rod had plucked one of his own guns from its holster, reversed it, and had struck the other hard on the back of his head. The man dropped like a sack without another sound.

Swiftly, without pausing to think, Rod moved towards the window. A quick glance was enough to tell him that the room beyond was empty. The man had been alone. It was the work of a few moments to climb inside. The main weight of fire seemed to be coming from the front of the house now where the Triple Star men had shifted their attack. It provided Rod with the opportunity he had been waiting for. Quickly, he moved over to the door, twisted the handle, opened it and peered cautiously out. There was a short corridor and at the moment it was empty.

He was halfway along it when a man appeared at the far end. For a moment, the other stared at him in stunned surprise and it was this momentary hesitation which cost him his life. Before he could make a move towards the guns in their holsters, Rod had whipped up his own gun and shot him twice at close range. The gunman died on his feet and a second later, Rod stepped over his still body, knowing that the shots would have been heard and Carswell might have guessed at their significance.

Listening intently at the door of one of the rooms, he thought he heard a faint movement inside. Grasping the handle, holding a sixgun tightly in the other hand, he jerked the door open and stepped through. Jeff Carswell stood at the window, his body flattened against the wall at one side. He was in the act of firing a quick snap shot through the window at a running man outside in the courtyard when Rod slipped into the room. Swiftly, instinctively, he jerked himself around, bringing up his gun as he did so. He was fast, dangerously fast, but Rod knew that he had shaded the other on the draw. His gun went off, deafening in the small room and the Colt went spinning from Carswell's smashed hand. The rancher reeled back against the wall, holding his shattered wrist, staring down at the blood which was trickling from it and dripping onto the floor from the ends of his fingers.

'Just stay right where you are, Carswell,' Rod said warningly. 'Most of your men have been either killed or wounded. This is the end for you and your rustling ways.'

'You won't hang me for cattle stealin',' said the other through his teeth, forcing a note of confidence into his tone. 'Try to get a jury in Twin Ranchos to convict me and see how far you get.'

'Could be that I'll act as judge and jury myself,' said Rod calmly. He went forward, pushed the other against the wall with the flat of his hand, then plucked the man's second gun from its holster and thrust it into his own belt. 'Now get outside and call on the rest of your men to stop firin'. We don't want to have to kill more than we have to and there ain't no sense any more of 'em dying for you. You're just not worth it.'

Carswell clamped his lips tightly shut. For a moment he seemed on the point of refusing, then he gasped with agony as Rod thrust the barrel of his gun hard into the other's stomach. He retched for a moment, swallowed, his face grey under the tan. Stepping to the window, he yelled thinly: 'Stop firin'. Wellman has got the drop on me.'

'That's better,' Rod said softly. 'Now you're showin' a little sense.'

'You'll pay for this, Wellman. I promise you that. Once we get into Twin Ranchos, you'll see who really has the upper hand. You'll be the one to swing from the end of a rope, I assure you.'

'You're talkin' too much again,' Rod said. He made the other move ahead of him, out of the house and into the dusty courtyard. Five men came out of the house with their hands lifted. From the hills surrounding the ranch, the Triple Star hands came down, their guns in their hands.

'So we got him alive,' said the foreman harshly. He stood in front of Carswell, eyeing the rancher up and down. He grinned broadly. 'I figure that with the evidence that Wellman can produce at your trial, you're as good as swingin' from the end of a rope right now.' He turned to Rod. 'Why don't we save ourselves the trouble of takin' them back into town. We could hang 'em all right now.'

'They'll get a fair trial,' Rod said sharply. 'Even though they don't deserve it. They wouldn't do the same if the positions were reversed, I know. But if there is ever to be any law and order in Twin Ranchos again, as there was when my brother was alive, then we have to do things this way.'

'You think that Charlie Ferris will carry out any order to hang Carswell?' said the other thickly. 'He's in cahoots with this *hombre*.'

'I know that,' Rod nodded. 'When we get back into

town, I figure we ought to relieve Ferris of his post and appoint a Sheriff who can be trusted to see that the law is carried out. We can have a word with Mayor Kerby on that point once we've got these *hombres* back safely.'

It was dark by the time they rode into town but there were lights all the way along the street and Rod saw several of the folk on the boardwalks eyeing them and their prisoners curiously. All the time they had been riding from the ranch, Rod had felt both vaguely puzzled and a little uneasy by the assurance of Jeff Carswell. Somehow, the other felt sure that he would not hang in spite of what he had done, in spite of any evidence that Rod might be able to bring against him. Inwardly, he felt troubled. Just what did the rancher have up his sleeve in town? It had to be something more than merely relying on Ferris to refuse to carry out Rod's order to arrest Carswell and the men with him on a charge of rustling. Did Carswell think that by now, Ferris would have discovered the evidence and destroyed it? Rod debated that possibility in his mind, then decided that it was something more concrete than that.

The party reined up in front of the Sheriff's office and a moment later the door opened and Charlie Ferris stepped out on to the boardwalk. For a moment he stared up at them in stunned surprise, his gaze flickering from Rod to Carswell and back again. Finally, he found his voice. 'What is this, Wellman?'

'I've brought Jeff Carswell in on a charge of rustlin' cattle,' Rod said sharply. 'I've also got the evidence to prove what I say.'

'Now see here,' said Ferris. 'I know you rode into this town with a chip on your shoulder, blamin' everybody for killin' your brother, and I guess you had a right to feel sore, but when you start goin' around accusin' men like Mr Carswell of rustling then you've got to have some pretty strong evidence to back up that charge and somehow I don't figure you've got that evidence. Seems to me though, that Mr Carswell could make a good charge against you.'

'I don't doubt it,' said Rod grimly. 'Such as shooting up his ranch and killin' off several of his crew. Only this time, there's going to be a decent kind of law in Twin Ranchos, not the kind that you deal out, taking your orders from Carswell. You're in this up to your neck too, Ferris. We don't recognize you as representin' the law any longer.'

The veins in the other's neck swelled visibly at that. For a second, his hands hovered above the guns in his belt, then froze there as Rod's voice cut through the stillness like the lash of a whip. 'Just try to make play for your guns, Ferris. I'll enjoy shootin' down a dirty polecat like you. If there is anythin' I hate more than a rustler, it's a dirty, two-timing lawman who hides behind that star of his and pulls every dirty trick in the book.'

'You can't get away with this, Wellman. So your brother was the Sheriff here, but that don't give you the right to take his place. I'm the duly elected representative of the law here and only Mayor Kerby can change that.'

'Then maybe we'd better have a word with the Mayor,' said Rod evenly. 'But in the meantime, we're puttin' Carswell and the rest of his boys in jail. And I figure we'd better do the same about you.'

For a moment, it looked as though in spite of everything, Ferris intended to go for his guns. The sweat stood out on his forehead and his hands were clawed by his sides. Rod sat in the saddle, waiting, not once removing his eyes from the other. Ferris stared at him tightly for a long moment, then sucked air into his lungs and relaxed visibly, keeping his hands well away from his sides.

'That's better,' Rod said keenly. 'For a minute there, I figured you were all set to take a short trip to Boot Hill.'

He stepped down from his horse and walked up to the other, jerked both guns from the man's belt and tossed them onto the ground near the boardwalk. 'Now get back inside,' he said thinly. 'We'll see how you like a taste of your own jail.'

Ferris drew back his lips over his teeth, but said nothing and after a brief moment, he turned and went inside the office. The keys to the cells hung on a large iron ring, near the door. Reaching for them, Rod waited in the doorway and motioned to the men to bring the other prisoners inside. 'Once we get them all locked up, we'll have a word with Kerby. I don't doubt that he's still awake, even at this time of night.'

'You figure he'll do as you ask and agree to have them locked away here?' asked the girl.

'Don't know of any reason why he shouldn't. After all, if he wants to be Mayor again, he'll need the vote of the townsfolk and they're more likely to vote for a man who showed that he could stand up for law and order, than one who bowed down to Carswell.'

Julie nodded, but did not seem to be really convinced. Herding the men into the cells at the rear of the building, Rod locked the doors, then went out into the office. He tossed the bunch of keys onto the table. 'I guess that takes care of that,' he said, a trace of weariness in his voice. 'I'll keep a watch here. A couple of you try to find Kerby. The rest of you had better get some rest. It's been a hard day.'

'I'll get the Mayor,' Julie said. 'I think I know where to find him.'

Rod nodded. The rest of the men followed on the girl's heels. He reckoned they would make for one of the saloons, slaking their thirst, washing the dust of the long journey out of their throats before they had any thought of sleep. He settled himself in the chair behind the desk, rested his feet on the polished top, leaning back and relaxing his body, although it was almost impossible for him to relax his mind. There were far too many questions still buzzing around in his brain, each demanding an answer, urgent and insistent. He had expected both Ferris and Carswell to make more of a fight of it, but they had gone into the cells as docilely as lambs and there had still been that sneering grin on the rancher's face as Rod had closed the cell door and locked it securely. Just what had the other on his mind that made him so confident he would not hang? Was he thinking that the rest of his men would arrive in time to prevent it? Rod remembered that Carswell had mentioned that half of his force had been away from the ranch. That could be it, he thought. But if they succeeded in destroying the force which Carswell had had with him at the ranch, there was every possibility that they could defeat this second bunch if they came riding into town, seeking to break Carswell out of jail.

He rolled himself a smoke and scowled at the opposite wall as he lit the cigarette. The uneasiness in his mind was something he could not dismiss, no matter how hard he tried. After a while, he got to his feet and walked around the side of the desk. He was still standing there, resting one hand on the top of the desk, when he heard the light step outside the door. A moment later, it was pushed open and the stout figure of Mayor Kerby came into the room. He stood for a moment blinking against the light, then he said softly: 'I heard that you had ridden into town with Jeff Carswell, Wellman? Where is he now?'

Rod pushed himself away from the desk, looked into the other's smoothly, bland features. 'I've got him and those men of his who are still alive, looked away in the cells. Ferris is with them.'

'Charlie Ferris?' Kerby opened his eyes wide. 'But why?'

'He's in cahoots with Carswell, has been from the beginning. I found some papers that my brother had left, tucked away in a secret compartment in one of the drawers to this desk. They implicate them all. We fought it out with Carswell this afternoon.'

' "We"?' inquired the other mildly.

'The men of the Triple Star ranch. Carswell himself had boasted to me that he would crush Julie Saunders as soon as the rest of his men rode into the ranch. We decided to hit him before he had the chance.'

'And the men of the Triple Star. Where are they now?' Kerby advanced into the middle of the room, looking about him.

'They'll no doubt be in one of the saloons, washing away the dust of the trail by now,' he said.

Kerby gave a broad smile. He withdrew his hand from the pocket of his frock coat. There was a small Derringer held firmly in his podgy fist and it was pointed straight at Rod's chest. 'Excellent,' he murmured. 'That was really all I wanted to know. Now we'll go back there and let Carswell and the other's out and if you make any move towards your guns, I'll shoot you down as I did your brother!'

Several seconds fled by before the other's words penetrated Rod's numbed brain. He stared at the Mayor as if really seeing him for the first time. 'So it was you,' he said harshly. 'You were the coyote who shot him down without a chance.'

'That's right. He discovered that I was the one who gave the orders here. He could have made things very awkward for me. So he had to die. Now get those keys and we'll turn those men loose. After that, I'll have to decide what to do with you.'

Rod clenched his hands helplessly by his sides. He knew it was useless to try to make a play for his own guns. The other's hand was as steady as a rock and it needed only one slight move for the other to squeeze the trigger of that small but very deadly weapon. Taking down the keys from the nail on the wall he walked in front of the other through the door at the back of the room and along the dimly lit corridor, pausing in front of the cell where Carswell was seated on the low bunk. The rancher glanced up, then got swiftly to his feet, lips thinned back, revealing his teeth as he recognized the man standing behind Rod.

'So you finally got here, Kerby,' he said. 'This *hombre* reckoned that he would hang us for those rustling jobs we pulled a couple of years back. Reckon he's now found out the real position.'

'Exactly,' murmured Kerby. He motioned with the Derringer. 'Unlock the door. Then we'll do the same for the others. I think that the Triple Star men will have a very unpleasant surprise waiting for them in a little while.'

Inside the cell, Carswell laughed harshly. 'Just let us get our hands on some guns and we'll smash them for good,' he boasted.

Rod paused, the keys still held in his hands. He knew that the moment he had let these men out, it would be the end for him, and for Julie and all of the decent citizens of Twin Ranchos. His mind was whirling desperately in his head, trying to figure out some way of stopping this, but there seemed no way of preventing these men from taking the Triple Star men by surprise. It would be all over before they knew what had hit them.

'Get a move on,' snapped Kerby, moving forward a pace. He waved the gun threateningly. 'We don't have all night to wait. Or would you rather I shot you down now and let them out myself?'

Rod stepped forward, inserted the key in the lock of the cell door. He saw Carswell's grinning face in front of him as the other came forward. Then, abruptly, shattering the clinging silence in the corridor, the revolver shot sent echoes shrieking between the walls. Rod jerked himself upright, whirled, dragging the key from the lock. Kerby stood against the far side of the corridor, his massive shoulders against the wall, his face a study of shock and surprise. The Derringer fell from his fingers and he was clutching his chest, a look of vacant bewilderment on his flabby features. He tried to turn his head, to peer along the corridor from where the shot had come, but could not quite finish the movement before his knees gave way under him and he flopped heavily onto his face at Rod's feet.

Julie Saunders came forward, staring down at him. Rod went to her and took the gun from her limp fingers. She said shakily: 'I couldn't find Kerby and I came back to tell you he was nowhere around. When I saw that you weren't in the outer office, I came here to look for you and heard Kerby talking just before I reached the door. I heard enough to realize what he had been doing. Was he the one who shot your brother?'

'Yes.' Rod nodded slowly. He placed his arm around the

girl's shoulders and gently helped her back along the corridor and into the office. 'He shot Hank because he'd found out that Kerby was mixed up in some of the shady deals in the town. I think we'll find plenty of evidence that Kerby got a lot of the money from the steers that were rustled from your ranch and sold. He probably had a big share in the saloons and gambling houses in the town.'

'And what will happen to Carswell and the others?'

'They'll get their trial and be sentenced as soon as the circuit judge gets here. I don't think there'll be much doubt as to their guilt. Maybe one of them will decide to talk and save us the trouble of finding any fresh evidence.'

'It all seems like a bad dream,' Julie said. 'And what about Rod Wellman? What will he do now that it's all over and his brother has been avenged?'

Rod shrugged. 'I don't know. Now that it's finished, I haven't any plans. Just keep on ridin' I suppose. Maybe I'll find someplace where I can settle down one day.'

'I need somebody on the ranch,' said the girl hesitantly. 'It needs a man to manage it. A woman can only do so much.'

'You offerin' me the job of foreman?' Rod looked towards her, with the lamplight shining on her face. There was a look there which he had not seen before. She was smiling at him, her eyes aglow. He saw a little of the colour come to her face. 'I was actually thinking of something more than a foreman,' she said simply.

The way she said it struck him powerfully, so that he could not wait for her to say anything more. He saw her lips tremble a little and wait – and it was like a great burst of heat going through him as he kissed her.